poetry, mystery
and

More

an anthology by
Ozarks Romance Authors Members

Margarite Stever – Joyce Smith
Wanda Fittro – Sharon Kizziah–Holmes
Janet K. Gallagher – Nancy B. Dailey
Lois Curran – Shirley McCann – S. J. Mais

Publishing Coordinator – Sharon Kizziah-Holmes

Paperback-Press
an imprint of A & S Publishing
A & S Holmes, Inc.

ISBN -13: 978-1-956806-39-7

DEDICATION

To the members of Ozarks Romance Authors.
Thank you for sticking with ORA during the
pandemic. Your loyalty is greatly appreciated.

ACKNOWLEDGMENTS

Thanks to Ozarks Romance Authors for allowing the writers in this anthology the opportunity to become published.

CONTENTS

INTRODUCTION

ORA was established in 1987. Today, we proudly embrace the legacy established by our founding mother, Weta Nichols, and are glad to offer an encouraging place for local authors to gather, share, and network.

Our members can be found across a multitude of genres, including mystery, mainstream, Christian romance, inspirational, YA, paranormal, sci-fi, memoirs, non-fiction and many more. Naturally, we welcome romance writers of all subgenres and heat levels. Whether you like it sweet or raunchy, you have a home at ORA.

Our members work hard to support each other and are proud to do so. Our writers loop helps us keep in touch with the group daily with publishing news, personal news, writing tips, and by simply building our friendship throughout the years.

Ozarks Romance Authors would like to invite you to join the fun, and we do have fun. If you've always wanted to write but never thought you could and/or just haven't tried, now's the time. We encourage you to follow that dream.

Feel free to contact us at
ozarksromanceauthors@gmail.com
for more details.
https://ozarksromance.com

MARGARITE R. STEVER

．▶▶◂◀▸

Margarite R. Stever grew up in Asbury, a tiny Missouri town of just over 200 people. She has a Bachelor of Arts Degree in English from Missouri Southern State University. She writes stories and essays that touch a person's heart. She is a member of Joplin Writers' Guild, Missouri Writers Guild, Sleuths' Ink Mystery Writers, Ozarks Writers League, and Ozarks Romance Authors. Her work has recently appeared in *Chicken Soup for the Soul: It's Beginning to Look a Lot Like Christmas;* Joplin Writers' Guild Anthology, *Seasons of the Four States; Anthology 2019 Sleuths' Ink Mystery Writers*; *Missouri's Emerging Writers*; *Legends: Passion Pages*; *50-Word Stories* website; the 2021, 2019, 2018, 2017, and 2016 issues of *The Crowder Quill;* the Fall 2015 issue of *The Maine Review; Mamalode Magazine's 2015 Better Together;* and *Writer's Digest 2014 Show Us Your Shorts Collection.* Her seeds of wisdom and joy can be read at ozarksmaven.com, which has been read in over 80 countries.

BECKY'S VALENTINE

Becky stopped in the middle of the dirt road and stared at the water raging across it in angry currents. For the third time, she shoved the car in reverse and turned around. She'd forgotten how this area flooded after a heavy rain. Her city posted blockades and warning signs any time a road closed. Out here in the country, there were no blockades or helpful signs.

Wind blew small tree limbs down in front of her as the muddy backroad sucked at her tires. A wild turkey took flight as she approached its resting place in the middle of the rarely travelled lane, which wasn't much more than a path. She stopped within sight of her sister's road and watched the angry creek gobble up the intersection.

Struggling to keep her car on the narrow dirt space, she reversed, spun the wheel, and then rocked forward again until she faced the way she'd come. She backtracked to where the muddy thoroughfare intersected another county route. With a small prayer, she turned right.

When she finally reached a highway and turned toward her destination, she cringed at a sign that read, "Impassable During High Water". The creek was high, but it wasn't over that bridge.

Despite the warning, she eased forward and headed toward her sister's place. She was happy to find a clear way to the narrow blacktop backroad she'd been trying so hard to access. Finally on the right road, she made good time to the farm.

Finding no mail in the box, she bounced down the muddy driveway and parked beside the ancient farmhouse. Her main reason for the trek stood and padded toward her, tail wagging.

"Hi, Gustaf. How're you doin' today, boy?"

She gathered her things and lugged them to the house. She let herself in with the spare key, then snagged the heavy-duty leash by the door and went back outside.

Gustaf reared up on his hind legs and pawed the air. "Get down. I can't put this on you with you jumping around." She clipped the leash to the German Shepard's collar, releasing him from the outdoor run where he stayed attached most of the time.

The moment the dog realized he was on the leash, he took off for the house, dragging her with him. He stopped in the kitchen and offered his neck so she could remove his leash. Then he galloped around the place before returning to poke his nose in her bag where he knew a treat was hiding. With a grin, she unwrapped the chicken flavored chew bone and offered it to him.

Picking up the note Liz had left on the kitchen table, she read her sister's explanation of the importance of bringing the mail inside every day due to a recent string of thefts. It went on to say Gustaf was allowed in the house under close supervision and should go back outside when she left. The rest of the note explained where she'd find various things she may need. Finally, it thanked her for taking care of things and wished her a Happy Valentine's Day.

"Yeah," she said to the dog, "it'll be happy because you're my Valentine this year. Who needs a man to love when you can have a dog?"

Opening her laptop, she settled at the kitchen table, anxious for a few hours of undisturbed writing. She'd only written three pages when Gustaf rushed to the back door and barked.

Her heart raced at the sudden intrusion on her silence. She'd never heard that dog bark in all the years she'd known him. She studied her canine friend. His hackles weren't raised, and he wasn't snarling. This was a happy bark.

"Someone here?" He wagged his tail and continued being vocal.

She was about to peek out the window when a sharp knock made her jump.

"Who is it?" she called.

"Liz, it's Lee Reynolds. I need to borrow something."

She stopped breathing for a moment. Lee was her high school sweetheart. The man who'd broken her heart so long ago. He'd joined the Air Force when she went to college and forgot all about her.

Smoothing her hair, she opened the door. Lee hadn't changed much since high school. He was still solid muscle. There were little creases around his blue eyes, and his sandy blond hair was streaked with silver. He was still the most handsome guy she'd ever seen.

"I'm afraid Liz isn't here. You'll have to settle for me." She tried to control the blush she knew was coloring her cheeks.

He stared at her for a moment before breaking into a huge grin. "Becky, is that you?"

"Yeah, in the flesh. How are you, Lee?" She opened the door wider. "Come on in."

"Can't complain too much. What in the world are you doing here at Liz's?"

Her temper flared a bit. "She's my sister. I take care of the place when she travels."

"Well, it's sure good to see you. I don't think I've laid eyes on you since right after our high school graduation." He looked her over with an interest that made her heart race. "You look great. Almost the same. Your brown hair looks nice streaked with silver, and those big brown eyes of yours are just as expressive as they ever were. I swear I can almost see your soul."

He stopped and coughed as if he couldn't believe he'd just said so much. Clearing his throat, he said, "I heard you were some famous writer or something."

"Famous? No. A writer? Yes. I've enjoyed some success, but not enough to quit my day job. I'm an accountant." She peered up at him from beneath her lashes, trying to hide the old feelings rising to the surface. "So, what do you do for a living?"

He shoved his hands in his pockets. "I'm a mechanic, and I farm. Like with your writing, I can't make it with just farming. The price of soybeans is at an all-time low. Corn isn't much better. I barely break even some years, but it's in my blood."

She nodded, trying to avoid the tingle rushing through her body at his closeness. "You said you needed to borrow something. How can I help?"

"Yeah, I need Liz's chainsaw. I bent the chain on mine. The storm blew down an old elm tree across my driveway. I need to be able to get to work tomorrow."

"The chainsaw is in the shed. I'll get the key." She lifted a ring of keys from a hook on the wall and headed outside.

Her old flame leaned his six-foot frame on the side of the shed. She could feel him studying her while she searched for the right key.

Opening the shed door, she pointed to the chainsaw. "There you go. Please don't break it, or Liz won't ever let me housesit again."

He laughed from deep inside. "No need to worry. I've been using one of these since I could lift it. I'll bring this back soon. Thanks a lot, Becky."

She watched his broad shoulders disappear down the muddy driveway as she tried to calm her thundering heart. Locking the shed, she returned to the house where Gustaf was watching her from a window. Lightning forked across the sky followed by a deafening clap of thunder. The frightened dog bolted outside the moment she opened the door.

"No! Gustaf, come back!" She chased him through the mud and muck as he dashed across a field. His long legs easily leapt over obstacles as the gap between them widened.

She lost sight of the runaway pooch and knew she had to find him before something bad happened. She was nearing panic when she heard a giant splash. She pushed herself to her limit, running faster than she ever knew she could. She stopped short of falling into the rain-swollen creek that had spilled over its banks onto the fields.

She heard a whimper over the roaring water. Visually searching the area, she spotted him a few yards away. He was balanced on a fallen tree that teetered above the rushing water.

She hurried to the part of the tree still on land and held out her hand. "Come on, boy. You can do it."

He hunkered down lower, trembling. She put one foot on the log and eased her weight onto it. Strong arms encircled her waist and lifted her off the fallen tree. She spun around the moment her feet touched the ground.

"What do you think you're doing? Can't you see I have to rescue the dog?" Her angry gaze clashed with Lee's fiery one.

He grasped her shoulders. "Are you crazy? That water isn't anything to play with. If you fall in, the current is sure to pull you under."

"I won't leave Gustaf there. Get out of my way!" She tried to pull free, but he held her fast.

"I'll get him. He might come to me since I'm calmer than you. Stay put, and I'll try." He released her and turned his attention to the dog.

He patted his chest. "Come on, boy. Come see me."

Gustaf whined before crawling to Lee. Becky sank to her knees and wrapped her arms around the wet dog, tears flowing from her eyes. "You scared me half to death."

She let the pooch lick her face as she hooked her fingers under his collar and stood. Turning to Lee, she swallowed the lump from her throat.

"Thank you. The thunder scared him, and he ran out when I opened the door. When I saw him hanging over the water like that, my only thought was to rescue him."

Lee cupped her cheek and tilted her face toward his. "You scared a good ten years off my life. I just found you again. I sure don't want to lose you now."

His declaration made her tummy flutter. "What do you mean?"

"I've always loved you, Becky. I'd planned to come back for you after I finished with Basic Training, but you were gone when I got home. Off to some fancy school to make something of yourself."

She fought to keep her emotions under control. "You never said anything about wanting to continue our relationship. You told me you were leaving and hoped I had a good life. I don't care how you spin it, that's a breakup line."

"I've never been good with words. I'm sorry." He ducked his head for a moment. When he looked at her again, determination sparked in his eyes. "What do you say I make you dinner tonight and we talk about it?"

"A date?" She studied him for a moment and

deemed him sincere. "That sounds good."

He smiled and brushed his lips against hers in a sweet kiss full of promises. He pulled back for a moment and then took her mouth again, showing her all of his long-simmering passion. When they parted, both were gasping for breath.

Lee's deep voice penetrated her foggy brain. "Becky, will you be my Valentine?"

Her heart nearly exploded in her chest. "I would love to."

CRUSHED BY MEDIOCRITY

I am crushed by mediocrity,
Oppressed by the average bear.
I choke on unrealized potential,
Mourn my untapped talent.

I yearn for unfulfilled dreams
While trampled by obscurity.
Reality encroaches on my world.
Such a brutal, evil master.

I must live in the mundane.
Wretched existence required.
I must toil to pay my way.
Drudgery strips me of my luster.

What then of my spirit,
So weary and so worn?
I have lost all of my fire
Fighting this battle called life.

GROWING OLD GRACEFULLY

Something very strange is happening to me.
I don't think I'm growing old gracefully.
I pee my pants when I sneeze. I pee my pants when
I sneeze!
To make matters worse, I have allergies!

My triceps seem to want to reach toward my knees.
My joints pop and my muscles freeze.
My hands ache when I type, and writing isn't a
breeze.
I feel a mid-life crisis creeping up on me.

Something very strange is happening to me.
I don't think I'm growing old gracefully.
I pee my pants when I sneeze. I pee my pants when
I sneeze!
To make matters worse, I have allergies!

I think my sight is going because I can't seem to
read.
When the air conditioning is on, I just about freeze.
I forget where I'm going, and I can't find my keys.
Can someone find a way to help me, please?

Something very strange is happening to me.
I don't think I'm growing old gracefully.
I pee my pants when I sneeze. I pee my pants when
I sneeze!
To make matters worse, I have allergies!

LOVE'S DESTRUCTION

Am I a rug for you to tread upon?
Do I lie listlessly on the floor?
Consider your actions or I will be gone.
Perhaps then you will want me more.

Your lack of respect is annoying.
At me you are always snapping.
Our bond you are surely destroying.
I think you need a good slapping.

I sacrifice for you and yours.
Yet I am still just an outsider.
I am an afterthought. No more.
You only want me as a provider.

Perhaps I will leave you now.
Will you even notice if I flee?
How much time should I allow?
You do not really even see me.

ROOSTER ON THE LOOSE

"**Q**uit that!" I yelled at the red rooster pecking at my heels and calves. I ran to my door, heavy grocery bags weighing me down as they swung from my arms.

He crowed at me, puffed out his hackles, flapped his wings, gnashed his beak, and extended his talons. He launched straight at my face. I dodged, but he caught his talons in my long brown hair, yanking a fistful out with his momentum. That hurt bad enough I saw stars. This had to stop.

I ran for the house in a haze of pain. He grazed my leg while I was unlocking the door, but I managed to keep him from taking a pound of flesh. Slamming the door behind me, I reached for my cell phone.

"Deer Crossing Police Department, how may I direct your call?"

"Someone dumped two hens and a rooster in my yard last week. I don't mind the hens, but the rooster chases me," I blurted. "I'm bleeding all over my kitchen floor from his latest attack."

"I'm sorry, but our animal control officer won't be in until Monday," the dispatcher replied.

"Please, can you send anyone to help? Anyone? I don't care if this fiend ends up on a farm or in a frying pan. I just want him gone! If I could just have the rooster removed, I won't complain about the hens. I'll even feed them and give them names. Just please help me get rid of this rooster from hell."

She sighed. "All right. I'll see if I can find someone."

"Thank you. I really appreciate your help."

A few minutes later, the doorbell rang. I answered it to a young muscular officer with a cocky grin. His ice blue eyes held confidence as his sandy blond hair rustled in the breeze.

"Jade Thompson? I'm Officer Shawn Tyndall. I understand you have a fowl problem." His expression remained professional.

"A severe fowl problem. Come to my backyard where the poultry play."

He grinned. I could tell he thought this would be easy. He didn't know this rooster, though. I led him through the house to the back door and nudged it open. The demon rooster was lying in wait.

"I should have this issue resolved momentarily," Officer Tyndall said with a smirk.

"Is your life insurance current?" I asked.

"Why?"

"Because that rooster is evil. He's going to teach you the meaning of pain."

He cocked a brow. "I graduated the academy at the top of my class. I should be able to handle one bad chicken."

I watched him take his first step out the door. The moment his boot hit my back step, the rooster attacked. Eyes swirling, he beat the poor guy with his wings and carved hunks of flesh from his thighs.

"Yow!" Officer Tyndall leapt back inside. "What was that?"

"The rooster from hell. I call him Lucifer." I pulled up my pant leg to show him my wounds.

He bent close and softly touched one nasty gash. "You should get this checked. You might need stitches."

"I'll survive. He took chunks out of you, too." I gestured toward his torn pants.

"All in the line of duty. We need a new plan." He thought for a moment before his beautiful eyes brightened. "Do you have a pillowcase I can borrow?"

"Borrow, no. Have, yes. I think I know your idea, and I don't want it back after Lucifer gets through with it."

He grinned. "This is going to work. I'll have this rooster out of here in no time. You said the hens are okay to stay until Monday, right?"

I went to the linen closet and grabbed a pillowcase. "If you can get rid of the rooster, those two hens can stay here forever."

He accepted the pillowcase and peered out the window. "Here's my plan. I'll walk out the door and wait for his attack. Then I'll catch him in the pillowcase and take him away."

"Where will you take him?"

"I'll set him free in the woods like I do the snakes I catch." He puffed out his chest.

I grabbed another pillowcase. "I'll hold onto this one in the event you need my help. That way, we can double-team him if we have to."

He nodded and peeked out the window. Lucifer was staring at the door. Taking a deep breath, the hero rushed outside. The rooster was on him before he had taken two steps. He tried to trap him, but the fowl was too quick.

I snuck out the front door and went around the side of the house where neither man nor rooster could see me. Creeping up on their showdown, I slammed my pillowcase over the rooster's head. His wings and talons were a frenzy of motion.

"Use your case to capture his feet," I yelled.

Officer Tyndall slipped the pillowcase beneath the rooster, capturing his feet. I wrestled my case down over the bird's wings. We tied the ends together in several places and rushed our burden to the front yard.

Lucifer was making enough noise to wake the dead. We carried him to the car where the officer popped the trunk.

"You want to put him in there? Are you sure that's a good idea?" I asked.

"You got a better one?"

I shook my head and watched him close the trunk. My imagination ran rampant with what he would find when he opened it.

"Maybe I should go with you. You might need help."

He looked down at his pants, then back up at me. "You may be right. I could use some backup, and I won't get any from the station. My sergeant told me not to come. He said we aren't rooster wranglers, and you'd survive until Monday. I was sure I could take care of this by myself."

My heart swelled. This brave officer had gone against his superior's wishes to rescue me. He was in for some serious ribbing just from the condition of his uniform. If he called and asked for help, they'd not only turn him down, but laugh at him as well.

I opened the passenger door of the patrol car and made myself comfortable. "I'm ready when you are, Officer."

He smiled at me. "You're brave and maybe just a touch crazy. I like that. You can call me Shawn." He put the car in gear and headed toward a nearby wooded area.

"You can call me Jade." I laughed a little too loud, just this side of hysterical. "You realize we're about to get our butts handed to us by a rooster, don't you?"

Shawn laughed, too. "Oh yeah. At least since there's two of us, we stand a chance of surviving. Why is that bird so mean? I thought chickens were supposed to be docile creatures."

"I've done some research since they arrived. I've discovered that chickens are considered prey animals, but some roosters get hormonal. They have a tremendous amount of testosterone for their size. His behavior is probably why the birds were dumped in the first place. Whoever had them couldn't handle Lucifer and decided to get rid of them all."

"I never thought about a chicken having hormones. Interesting. You learn something new every day." He pulled onto the side of the road near the woods.

"Do you think he'll be okay? What if one of those snakes you set loose out here decides he wants a chicken dinner?"

"Cold feet? I thought you didn't care if we set him free or fried him. Are you hiding a bleeding heart behind that tough exterior?" He chuckled as he headed for the trunk.

I followed him to the back of the car. "Okay, maybe I feel a little bad about dumping him out here after he was dumped at my house. I don't know what else to do with him. He's going to seriously hurt somebody."

"We aren't dumping him. He isn't a pet. He's an aggressive animal that should probably be put down. We're giving him a chance at freedom. Who knows? He might even calm down when he isn't around people anymore."

I considered his words as I listened to the commotion in his trunk. "He's really having a fit. What's your extraction plan?"

He stared at the car for a moment. "We'll pop the trunk and loosen the knots we used to tie the pillow cases together. Then we'll stand back while he works them apart. Once he's free, he'll fly off into the trees."

I regarded Shawn with wonder. He believed this would work. Since I didn't have a better idea, we went with his.

"Ready?" His gaze was steady on mine.

"Yeah, let's do this." I held my breath.

He popped the trunk, and Lucifer rained hell upon us. He'd slashed through the pillowcases and came up out of that trunk with death in his eyes. He flew at Shawn and got a good grip on his uniform shirt. Talons dug into Shawn's shirt, its beak like a pickaxe running at lightning speed. Feathers were flying everywhere from his wildly flapping wings. Shawn's face and neck were bloody in less than two seconds.

I whooped a battle cry and grasped the rooster's wings. I yanked him off my hero and flung him toward the woods. "Go to your new home before I ring your neck and put you in a pot!" I screamed at him. I bared my teeth and growled in my best predator impression.

Lucifer acted like he was coming for me but then thought better of it. He ran off into the woods making all sorts of noise.

I regarded Shawn with the blood running down his face and neck. His hair was standing up, and his pants were ripped beyond repair.

"Are you all right?"

He nodded. "I need to stop by my house to clean up before I go back to the station. I don't live far from here. Do you want to come with me, or would you rather I take you home first?"

"We should go to your house. Your wounds need cleaned and treated. I can help with that." I brushed a lock of silky hair off his forehead. "You've done battle today. None of your fellow officers will ever understand how much bravery this took or the extent of your injuries."

His grin was crooked. "They'll never find out. There's a steak dinner in this for you if it stays our little secret."

"Dinner? Are you asking me out on a date?" I teased.

His gaze turned intense. "Yeah, I think I am. Would you like to have dinner tonight?"

My smile fled. "I was just kidding. I wasn't hinting . . ."

"I know, but I really would like to take you out. I'd like to know more about the woman who rescued me from a demon rooster."

I could feel the heat in my cheeks and knew I was blushing. "Okay. That sounds good. Let's get you patched up so you can finish your shift first."

"Good idea." He closed the trunk and walked to the driver's door. "I get off work in a couple hours."

"It's a date." I slid into the passenger seat.

At his house, Shawn showered and dressed in a fresh uniform in less than ten minutes. I treated his wounds with ointment before he took me home.

"I'll pick you up around six o'clock, okay?"

"Sounds great." I smiled up at him. I kissed his cheek before I turned and went in the house.

I showered and treated my own wounds, paying special attention to the gash Shawn had mentioned earlier. I dressed in my best black jeans and a purple pullover. I was researching chicken coops when my doorbell rang.

Shawn looked great in his blue jeans and dark red t-shirt. The bleeding had stopped, but his gashes still looked angry.

"Hi. Come in."

"Thanks." He stepped inside and closed the door. He bent toward my computer and studied the screen with a grin. "Chicken coops? You're keeping the hens?"

"I don't know. They may decide to mosey on down the road now that their rooster is gone. If they stay, I think they should have a little place of their own."

He slipped his arms around me. "I can tell that this is going to be an interesting relationship. We'll be the cop and the chicken wrangler."

JOYCE VALDIOS SMITH

Joyce Valdois Smith is wife to Bob, mother to four married children, and grandmother to fourteen beautiful grandchildren. She is a retired public health nurse and school nurse. Writing has been her long-time passion. Joyce is an author of Christian historical fiction as well as children's books. She lives with her husband and Cavalier King Charles Spaniel, Lady Catherine (Katie), in southwest Missouri.

MISSOURI GOLD, RED GOLD THAT IS!

So this local fellow got plumb aggervated at his ornery hawgs. Took his muzzle-loader and filled it with seeds of the love apple [tomato] and shot at them hawgs. Them seeds took root and growed. When them plump, red 'maters was ripe, they felled off and rolled down the hillside, peeling 'emselves as they gathered speed. Bounced right into a boiling cauldron, and that how we knew we cud grow 'maters in these hills.

Robert McGill owns White Oak Press, near Reeds Spring, Missouri. This article first appeared in the book, In the Heart of Ozark Mountain Country, published by White Oak Press in 1992.

This bit of folklore illustrates the beginning of the tomato growing and canning business in Southwest Missouri. It was passed down through generations. Despite the implications of this facetious story, the business of growing tomatoes was anything but easy, yet it yielded an income to many early occupants of the Ozark region.

As early families began to settle the area in the late 1800s, they realized the rolling rocky hills were not conducive to the regular grain crops they may have grown before. They soon discovered that tomatoes and other fruit crops would flourish under these conditions. The Ozark hills provided abundant clear rushing streams from natural springs that flowed from the hillsides. And the settlers' large families provided the workforce to grow the tomatoes and work in the canneries which soon came into operation.

During the summer and fall of the first-year trees and brush had to be cleared from the hillsides. The north and east slopes were favored as the tomato plants would be partially shielded from the blazing afternoon summer sun. Everyone in the family would be put to work with cross-cut saws and chopping axes, cutting small saplings and bushes. The larger trees were girdled by stripping the bark around the trunk causing them to die. Then they would be cut down and burned. The stumps were dug out or blasted out with dynamite. When the ground was cleared the farmer would cultivate it with a mule-drawn two bottom plow to prepare the soil for planting in the spring. The more children in the family the better. They would be put to work gathering rocks and roots as the soil was worked. The plot was plowed on a four-foot grid as the tomato plants were planted four-foot apart.

In the spring, around the first of April, tomato seeds saved from the previous year were planted in a small patch of ground. An ideal location was where the brush had been burned as the heat from the fire killed the weeds so the seedlings could grow without competition. To protect from frost on cold nights, the farmer would cover the small plants with paper. Six weeks later, in the middle of May, when the spring sun had warmed the ground and the seedlings were about six inches tall, they were transplanted into the prepared fields. The tender plants were dug from the ground and bundled. Planting the tomatoes on the steep rocky slopes was time-consuming and backbreaking and was well suited to large families. One person would lay the plants at the intersections where the seedlings would be set. Other family members would poke holes in the ground with a small punch called a dibble, place the plant in the hole, and cover the roots with soil. An average field was about four acres. Rutger tomatoes were preferred as they adapted well to the hilly, rocky soil and were most desirable for canning.

The plants grew as the summer progressed. The farmers prayed for early summer rains and cultivated the soil around the plants with a mule and a cultivator to control weeds. The first green fruits appeared in early July and the pinkish-orange tomatoes developed by mid-August. The harvest extended into the cool weather of autumn. Family members who picked the fruit on the rocky hillsides during the intense August heat were motivated by the promise of reward for their efforts. Tomatoes were immediately transported to the canning factories where the growers were paid for their fruit.

In the 1890s small canneries began to operate around the Ozarks as investors realized the potential of this new industry. They began in the southern counties of Missouri and eventually spread over most of southwest Missouri from Webster County west and south. Many were in small towns and others were on private property, owned and operated by the individual families. Sparkling streams bubbled out of many hollows which provided clean water for washing, scalding, and cooking the tomatoes.

While the canning season was defined by hard work, it was also a festive, joyous time as family members, relatives, and friends, often from miles around, came together to work at the canneries. There was much laughter, camaraderie, and fun as they caught up on community gossip, family news, politics, and religion. Though laborers often lived in small, crowded shacks and tents, they anticipated the canning season. For some, picking and canning was their only source of income.

Some of the early canning operations were set up outside. Others were in makeshift buildings and barns. The farmer would deliver his crop by the wagon load, or later by truck, to the docks near the cannery. The tomatoes were emptied onto sorting tables where bruised or spoiled fruits were separated and discarded. They were then washed, placed in wire baskets, and lowered into scalding water to loosen the skins. Buckets of tomatoes were then sent down the line to the tables where women and girls waited on each side to peel and core them. The buildings were insufferably hot and humid as the August sun beat down and the cauldrons of boiling water sent steam into the air. Each woman peeled the tomatoes in her bucket, letting the peels fall into a trough in the middle of the table. By using an ultra-sharp skinning spoon, she could core then slip the tomatoes from the skin. If the skin stuck to the tomato she could use the sharp blade of the "tomato spoon" to cut it loose. The workers became adept at their task, but had to be careful as one slip of the sharp spoon could cause a gushing bloody wound. Each woman or girl received a token for every bucket she peeled. The tokens were redeemed at the end of the week for wages. The tomatoes were then moved to the canning area. They were pushed through a funnel into the opening in the top of the can. Early tomato cans were manufactured in eastern steel towns, such as Philadelphia, and shipped by rail to the nearest railroad. They were sealed at the manufacturer except for a small hole, two inches in diameter, in the top of the can. After the can was filled, the opening was soldered shut and the cans were placed in large round cookers to process them for several hours. They were then cooled, labeled and stacked ready for shipment.

Early canneries produced 500 to 1000 cans a year. As the equipment improved and the railroad expanded, industry buyers for food wholesale companies traveled from across the country to buy the canned tomatoes. The buyers scoured the countrysides in the fall for tomatoes and provided labels for their parent companies. The box loads of tomatoes would be shipped to stores across the nation and even to foreign countries. The Ozarks were responsible for a large part of the tomatoes eaten in the US from the 1910s through the 1940s and 1950s.

For years the tomato canning industry was a way of life for many southwest Missouri farmers. The industry supported the financial needs of their families and in turn the families built much of their social and community life around the tomato industry. There were over 300 canneries in operation in the 1930s.

New innovations--the use of fertilizer, hybrid seeds and tractors--which were more suited to large fields in California and Florida than to small hillside patches in the Ozarks led to the demise of the tomato canneries in Missouri. Inside the canneries newer more expensive equipment was needed to speed the process while federal regulations constantly upgraded sanitary requirements. Ozark canneries simply could not justify the massive expenditures needed to continue the business.

There was a resurgence during WWII, but once the war ended the canneries began to shut down. Canning factories situated near the railroad survived the longest, but many closed in the 1950s. The last canning factory in the area, in Taney County, was closed in 1968.

Many people find it difficult to believe the heavily forested Ozark hillsides were once tomato fields and that tomato canneries dotted the landscape. Yet it is an interesting reality of the Ozarks and Southwest Missouri's economy and history.

RED GOLD OZARK LOVE

Rachel Gardner blinked as sweat ran down her forehead and into her eye. She stepped away from the peeling table, pulled the handkerchief from her pocket, wiped her brow, and blew her nose. "Whew!! It must be a hundred ten degrees in here."

"I know. It's blazin' hot. I'm about to go up in a plume of smoke." Her best friend, Leah Hardinger, worked beside her in the local tomato factory. Their job was to peel tomatoes as they came down the conveyor belt from the scalding vats. Other women and girls from the community and surrounding area worked near them.

The late afternoon heat combined with the steam from the boiling vat made it hard to breathe. Although the sides of the building where they worked were open, there was little breeze to stir the air.

"Sister, wash your hands before you return to work!" Rachel's mom admonished from the next table where she assisted with filling tin cans.

Rachel hurried to the washing station where a barrel of water sat. A bar of lye soap and a towel lay near it. She turned the spigot, wet her hands, scrubbed them with soap then rinsed and dried them.

She scampered back to the table just in time to grab the two buckets headed toward her. One was filled with scalded tomatoes, the other was for the peeled tomatoes. With agile hands, she picked up her coring spoon and grabbed the first tomato. The peel slipped off, she gave the corer a flip then dropped the tomato in the empty bucket. The core and peel slipped into the trough at the center of the table. She emptied the bucket in time to grab the next two. She and Leah competed to see who could peel the most. They received a token for each bucket they completed. The tokens would be exchanged for cash at the end of the week.

A truck rumbled over the Missouri rock up the drive toward the cannery. That'd be another load of tomatoes from one of the surrounding farms. Rachel strained to see who was driving. Would it be Josh Wilson? He was their neighbor's oldest son. Her heart gave a jolt as she glimpsed his blond hair through the truck window. It was him. He was absolutely the most handsome man in the whole community. Tall with sandy, blond hair and the most gorgeous tan. His deep blue eyes sparkled with life and fun. He'd asked her out several times through the summer. It was difficult to keep her attention on tomatoes.

He drove the truck to the unloading dock and stepped out. Rachel allowed herself a few moments to stare at him. Her pulse rate increased. He was shirtless and his muscles rippled in the sun as he unloaded the baskets of tomatoes from his family's tomato patch.

"Get back to work." Leah's whisper drew Rachel's attention back to the job at hand. "It's not gonna do you any good to stare."

"I know, but I can't help it. I hope he invites me to the Fall Harvest Festival." Rachel resumed peeling. She had let Leah overtake her twice. She needed to concentrate.

Family, friends, and neighbors from miles around gathered to work at her parents' cannery every summer. The season ran from mid-August to the cool days of autumn. Now was the busiest time. A hum of conversation and occasional bursts of laughter filled the large metal building that housed the cannery. A low rumble reached her ears as another basket of tomatoes was emptied onto the sorting table. Spoiled and rotten tomatoes would be discarded, the rest were transferred to the huge boiling cauldron. The tomatoes were then distributed to the buckets and sent on the conveyor belt to the station where she and Leah and four others were peeling. Next, they were put in gallon cans, sealed, and heated in large canners to kill any harmful germs.

Rachel glanced up just in time to see Josh walk across the platform behind her to collect the money for the load of tomatoes he'd delivered. She returned her gaze to the job in front of her. Peel, core, plop, peel, core, plop. Rachel could hear her mother talking to Josh. She filled her bucket and passed it along, just in time to catch the next ones.

"Hi, beautiful. How's it going?"

Rachel jumped and nearly pushed the bucket of tomatoes over on the conveyor belt. "Josh, you startled me! I almost cut myself on my coring spoon."

"I'm sorry. I thought you knew I was there."

"I didn't know you'd come up behind me and scare the bejeebers out of me."

"I said, I'm sorry."

She grinned. "I know. It's alright."

He leaned over. "Meet me at the waterfall after supper. About eight o'clock, okay?"

Rachel blinked and stilled. She didn't want to turn around and catch her mother's attention. "Yes, okay, I'll meet you there."

"Good, I'll see you then." He stuffed his money in his pants pocket then turned and walked out of the building.

Rachel grabbed a tomato off her bucket and slipped the peel off. Her heart was doing a tap-dance. "Did you hear that? He asked me to meet him at the waterfall."

"Do you think I'm deaf? Of course, I heard. I wish Peter would ask me to meet him there."

"What should I wear?" Rachel attacked her bucket of tomatoes. They flew through her hands into the second container.

"Wear what you've got on."

Rachel wrinkled her nose. "This? You're kidding. It's nasty."

"He already saw you in it and called you beautiful. I don't think you have much to worry about."

"You aren't very romantic."

"Yes, I am. I just don't have anyone to be romantic with."

"I think Peter's going to ask you to go to the festival."

It'd be nice, but I'm not holding my breath."

Rachel sped up her pace. She'd have to work hard to reach her quota. Her dad wanted a hundred cans processed in a day.

After supper, Rachel hurried to help her mother clean the kitchen. She glanced at the mantle clock. It was fifteen minutes before eight. "Can the boys help with the dishes tonight? I want to go for a walk."

"Are you going to meet Josh?"

Rachel hesitated. "Yes, he asked me to meet him."

"Well, don't be late. Your dad doesn't like you out after dark."

"Okay." Rachel breathed a sigh of relief and rushed out the door before her mother could change her mind. Thank goodness, she'd washed her hands and face and changed into her best dress before supper. She strode up the path to the top of the hill. Springwater gushed out of a cave and fell in a magnificent waterfall into the stream below. The cannery had been built here on her dad's property because of this constant supply of water. It was used to process the tomatoes. Beside the waterfall, a large rock protruded out of the hillside. It was the perfect place to sit.

As she hiked closer, she could see Josh on the rock. She drew in her breath. The setting sun shone from behind him and made him look like a Greek god. His blond hair gleamed in the light. She was glad to see he'd put his shirt back on. He was too enticing without it.

He sat up as she approached. Then stood up and walked down to meet her. "I'm glad you came. This is the best time to be here." He took her hand and helped her over the rocks. "The view's magnificent. And the spray from the falls is refreshing." He grinned at her. "It was especially beautiful with you walking up the hill."

"You could see me?"

"Yes, you can see everything from here." He guided her around to the backside of the rock where it was easier to step up then indicated for her to sit with her back against another smaller rock. He sat beside her.

Rachel breathed in a deep breath and let it out slowly. "It's amazing up here." The tension and tiredness of the day dissipated, and she felt her shoulders relax.

They sat quietly for a few minutes as the tranquility of nature enveloped them. The green leaves of the trees threw patches of sunshine and shadow across the scene below them.

Josh put his arm around her. "Would you consider going to the Harvest Festival with me?"

She laughed softly. "Yes. I hoped you'd ask."

"I have another question." He faced her. "Would you marry me?"

Rachel whirled around. "Josh, do you mean it? You want me to marry you?"

"Yes, I've wanted to ask you for a long time. I've made enough with the tomato harvest to get us a small place."

"Oh, Josh, yes. Yes, I'll marry you." She felt his body warmth as he pulled her toward him. Joy and ecstasy flowed through her at the touch of his lips. Her body responded as she returned his kiss. The red gold summer beauty surrounded them as they lost themselves in young love.

WANDA FITTRO

Wanda Fittro lives in the beautiful Ozark Mountains in Southwest Missouri. She won the prestigious Missouri Literary Festival Reader's Choice award in 2011 for her Civil War short story One, Two, Three. You can find her novel Beyond The Horizon on Amazon.

THE SABBAT

‎T‎he ceremony had just begun when lightning raced across the sky. Shelly was glad she decided to move the monthly Sabbat into the barn because of the weather forecast. She left the barn doors open so if the weather did clear up, they could get the full effect of the moon. They had some important work to do tonight.

She was a fairly new high priestess, having completed the rigorous training just a few months earlier. Three years and three days was a long time to devote to something, but it was in her blood. She came from a long line of witches. Some solitary, some in covens. She was the first high priestess in her family. Something she didn't take lightly.

Her coven was a mixture of old and young, each one with their own special gift. Which, Shelly was thankful for. Running a coven was no easy task and the more help she could count on the better. There were currently nine members. Thirteen was the ideal number. But they needed to be picky when it came to allowing somebody to join them. Shelly learned that the hard way.

The coven had just created their circle by calling

on the spirits of Earth, Wind, Fire, and Water, when three shadowy figures appeared in the doorway. Another snap of lightning spread across the sky. One of the figures cleared his throat bringing Shelly's attention out of their circle of power. She saw the glimmer of a badge.

"Jean, take over." Shelly backed out of the circle knowing she couldn't return that night. Once you leave a circle, it's best not to return and disturb the power created. Not wanting the interruption to stop the ceremony, she rushed to the door and indicated the men to follow her outside. She raised the hood on her cloak against the wind and led the men to an attached lean-to where farm equipment lined the wall.

"Sheriff, I don't appreciate this interruption of our Sabbat. I can't imagine you would interrupt the First Baptist Church service like this." Shelly couldn't miss the smirk on his face.

"I would hardly compare this, uh, gathering, to Pastor Wilson's congregation."

Shelly glared at him. "We are protected by the First Amendment also, whether some of the good folk of this town want to believe it or not."

"I'm not here to debate the constitution." He handed her a picture. "Do you recognize this person?"

The photo sent shock waves through her. She covered her mouth and shoved the picture back at the sheriff. "That's James." She choked back the urge to vomit. "What happened?"

"Why don't you tell us."

"How would I know?"

"Well, first off, one of your witch marks is carved into his chest. I think you all call it a pentagram."

"Sheriff, think about it. If myself or anybody else in the coven wanted to kill somebody, would we be stupid enough to leave such a clue?"

"If they wanted to make a statement." He adjusted his holster belt. "What about the history between you and the victim?"

Shelly hugged herself. "Yes, we had a relationship. But it ended amicably. I haven't seen him in months."

"We have a report that he was denied entry into your . . . um . . . coven. And he wasn't happy about that. Did he threaten you?"

"No, I explained to James that our group voted to keep our coven all female. It is important for women to feel protected and powerful and sometimes a male presence threatens that. He understood."

"So, some of your members felt threatened by him? Interesting."

"I didn't say that. Have you questioned Pastor Wilson?"

"Of course not. He is an upstanding member of our community. Why should we bring him into this?"

"Because he has threatened us on many occasions. He's stopped our members in town, waved the Bible at them, screaming for his god to bring his wrath down upon us. I'm telling you his mind is not right."

"So, you are suggesting Pastor Wilson would go

to this extreme to discredit you and your followers? That's ridiculous." He turned to his deputies. "Cuff her."

Just then, Pastor Wilson approached from the darkness. "Thank you, Jesus." He fell to his knees.

Shelly could only stare at the sight before her eyes. His robe was covered in blood. He held a bloody knife in his right hand and the Bible in his left. His eyes were glazed over and his mouth stretched into a bizarre grin. "The devil has met his match. Let him be vanquished from this peaceful community and this heathen woman be sent to hell to join him."

He slashed the sign of the crucifix on the front of his robe. "Your will be done."

THE TREASURE

"**H**ow did you lose your eye?"

"Wow, you don't beat around the bush, do you?" He brushed a loose strand of his long, wavey, black hair from his face.

Maggie took a sip of her Margarita and licked some salt off the rim. "I've been told that." Her thoughts raced to memories of her mother scolding her for being rude.

He adjusted the black patch covering his right eye. "I was on the short end of a sword fight."

"What are you, some sort of pirate?"

He leaned toward her. "Yes, but let's keep that between you and me."

"Aaarghh matey," she said and raised her arm in a pirate salute, fist clenched, arm bent at the elbow. Embarrassed, she slowly lowered her arm. Not a great impression on a first date. *Better lay off the Margaritas.*

She looked at her friend Stacey across the table who seemed to be embarrassed for her. Clearing her throat, she said, "Have you told Mark what you do for a living?" Before she could answer, Stacy looked at Mark and said, "Maggie works at

Disneyland on the Pirates of The Caribbean ride. Which explains her pirate talk."

Stacey had set this blind date up and Maggie was already doubting her decision to go along with it. In her experience, these things never panned out. But there was something about this man. A hint of mystery. And he was handsome in a swashbuckling sort of way. *Okay, maybe she was obsessed with her job.*

"Really? How fascinating. That's my favorite ride. What do you do?" Mark leaned in closer. His smell was intoxicating. A mixture of manliness and danger. She felt a bit dazed and took a minute to answer.

"Oh, a little bit of everything." She finally managed to choke out.

"You know what would be cool? If you could sneak me in and show me the inner workings. It's kind of a fantasy of mine. Also, I've heard there is actual pirate treasure hidden in there."

"That's just an old wife's tale. Not a bit of truth in it."

"Well, okay. But I still would love to get in there."

"I don't know. That is way against the rules. I could get fired or worse." She didn't mention she actually had snuck somebody in before. The night watchman at the rear entrance to the park had a thing for her. And she didn't mind using that to her advantage. She felt her cheeks blush at the memory of that night. A little role playing is always fun. And Mark did fit the bill of a pirate. "Oh, what the heck. Let's go!"

Maggie parked her car in the employee parking lot close to the rear entrance. She instructed Mark to slump down in the seat. "I'll distract him and when you see me motion, you sneak in the entrance."

Clyde, the night watchman, smiled when she walked up. "Hi Maggie. What are you doing here so late?" She reached for his tie and guided him away making sure his back was to her car and the entrance. "Oh, silly me forgot to check on a malfunctioning computer program before I left. Didn't realize it until I was home and getting ready for bed. I probably look a mess." As she talked, she motioned behind Clyde's back to Mark.

"Nah, you always look beautiful." He stroked her outstretched hand that was still holding his tie.

"Ah, thanks Clyde." She pulled her hand away. "I have to go now. I don't want to be here all night." She stepped around him, blew him a kiss, and entered the building.

When the door shut behind her, Mark jumped in front of her, grabbed her by the waist, and planted a quick kiss on her lips. "You are fantastic."

"Uhhh, umm," she stammered.

"I want to see the treasure room first."

"Don't you want to see how it all works?"

"Maybe later. I want to immerse myself in the scenes I love and who knows what may happen." He kissed the back of her hand.

Maggie held his arm as she maneuvered along the catwalk that swept behind the scenes. Only the recessed ceiling lights shined in the darkness. When they reached the treasure room, Maggie flipped a large switch on the wall. The whole scene lit up. No motion, no sound, just illumination.

Mark headed straight to the fake pile of gold treasure in front of one of the inanimate pirates. He moved his hands around the perimeter in a deliberate manner. She could tell he was searching for something.

"What are you doing?" she asked.

He didn't answer.

Maggie heard a loud click and the treasure pile moved to the left. Her mouth fell open as he pulled out an armored box.

"What the . . .?"

"My grandfather was on the construction crew and hid this as the ride was being built." He looked up. "He was a pirate. As am I."

Maggie couldn't speak. Her eyes widened as he removed a key hanging around his neck and opened up the treasure chest. The gold in the box glistened in the lights.

"Okay, okay, this is not happening." She backed away in shock.

"Oh, but Maggie my dear, it is happening." He pulled a long knife out of his boot. "And I'm truly sorry, but I can't leave a witness."

When the visitors left the ride the next day, they all remarked how realistic the scenery was, especially the dead woman in the treasure room with the knife sticking out of her chest.

SHARON KIZZIAH-HOLMES

▶▶ ◄◄

Sharon Kizziah-Holmes started writing songs in her teens and became an accomplished, professional musician. Although she continued to perform, her passion changed from music to writing fiction. After joining Ozarks Romance Authors in the early 1990s she attended conferences, seminars and workshops to hone her skills and learn the fundamentals of the writing and publishing industries. She gives writing classes on many subjects and likes teaching the basics of the penned word. Even more, she loves to help authors realize their publishing dream, so she started her own company. Paperback Press is an indie author services provider that offers everything from professional cover design, illustrators, paperback, e-book and children's book formatting to a finished product.

SPRINGTIME SNOW

Judith Cane sat at her desk and stared at the document on the laptop screen in front of her. The page silently glared back with only two words typed in the center, CHAPTER 15.

It had been three days since she'd written a single word. Frustration settled in, tears threatened to spill onto her cheek, and she began to type the first thing that came to mind. *Being a published romance author is totally overrated*! Then she slammed the computer shut, stood and went to her favorite chair.

The fire blazing in the hearth heated the room but did nothing to warm her chilly mood. "Boy, Charlie, I'm in a foul frame of mind today, aren't I?" Today and everyday, it seemed as of late. She bent and patted the canine atop the head then sat down and pulled a throw over her legs. "Tell me, how's a woman supposed to write a story about love and romance when *her* life is totally void of it?"

She couldn't help but smile when the old dog whined his protest. "I know you love me fella. I love you to, but I'm talking about love of the human kind. M A N being the three key letters in that word." Having Charlie there helped relieve some of her stress and she was grateful for that.

Gray clouds drifted across the sky above the Ozarks. The first day of spring had come over a week ago and that was just about how long it had been since she'd been out of the house. She swore if it snowed one more inch, she would absolutely scream.

She studied Charlie all cuddled up on his bed next to the fireplace. "You know what, buddy? Springtime's supposed to bring Lilacs, Black-eyed Susan's, Honeysuckle and green grass. Not snow." Man, she sounded like a pouting teenager. What was happening to her?

Her mind wandered back to her wedding day. At one time she'd loved Zachary Cane more than life itself. He'd been a great husband at first, then jealousy plagued him. So what if she made more money writing than he did as a bank executive. It didn't matter to her, she loved him.

However, it bothered him. He started drinking then lost his job and took it out on her. He'd said it was her fault that his life was going to hell. It wasn't, she knew it and refused to let him take her down with him.

The memories of good times and bad tugged at her heart. No wonder she was depressed. The only man she would ever love, or ever wanted to love, let the whiskey bottle take over his life. She couldn't compete with that.

Judith glanced around the beautiful room that surrounded her. She had once enjoyed being there with her husband, but at this point in time she wished Zach had the place stuck snugly up his nose.

The dog suddenly started to bark. Bang, clank! "What in the...?" Noises from outside penetrated the quiet of the evening. Clatter...crash!

Glancing out through the huge bay window of the living room she saw the solid white yard and driveway, but nothing else. Had a car crashed? "I have to hurry, Charlie, someone might be hurt."

Her coat went on easily then she pulled on boots, opened the front door and rushed onto the porch. Thankfully she'd shoveled snow from the walk the day before but beyond that it was a couple of feet deep. Looking up at the sky, she realized it was almost dusk. "We'd better get a flashlight, boy." Charlie panted with excitement as he followed her.

Back inside she checked the flashlight batteries. On her way back out she retrieved her cell phone from the kitchen counter. She didn't get great reception in the house, but from the main road she could call 911 if she needed to.

Charlie leaped over the snow toward the highway. Through the naked trees of winter, the faint glow of headlights moved slowly up her drive. "Charlie, come back here." Whoever had crashed must have been okay. At least the car was still drivable. But why wouldn't they go back to town instead of coming toward her house?

Realty struck and she realized her vulnerability. Taking a deep breath, she tried to slow her racing pulse. She had to get back to the house, quickly. "Charlie, come here." The canine hesitated then followed obediently.

At least she had her pepper spray for protection. A lump formed in her throat when she entered the house, then shut and locked the door. She was afraid. For the first time, she was scared of being alone.

The portable land line phone felt cool when she picked it up on the way to the bay window. After closing the blinds she peeked out at the car that, little by little, approached the house.

She dropped the blind slat back into place, stepped away and placed her hand to her throat. Closing her eyes, she took a deep breath. She couldn't have a panic attack, not right now. She needed to stay calm. It could mean the difference between life and death. "Come on, Judith, get it together."

Charlie's tail wagged as if nothing was wrong. Why hadn't she had the Labrador trained to be a guard dog? He'd be useless against an intruder.

The sound of the car motor came to an abrupt stop just outside the house. She ran into the bedroom, grabbed her pepper spray then hurried back to the window to look out.

The shadowed shape of a man got out of the car, but the dim light of dusk made it impossible to see the figure clearly. She thought she would stop breathing completely when she recognized the man who approached her door. "Zach?" What was he doing there? He was drunk. He had to be.

Fear turned to anger as she heard him stomp the snow from his feet at the front door. How dare he invade her privacy in his drunkenness?

"Charlie, stop wagging your tail. He's not going

to be here long, so don't act like you're happy to see him. You hear me." Little good her scolding did. Her supposed *best friend* ignored her. "Fine."

She went to the door and jerked it open before Zach could ring the doorbell. She glared at him. His eyes were bright and his six-foot two frame stood tall and steady. Was he sober? No, she didn't dare have hope of that.

Locking the glass outer door between them she asked, "What do you want, Zach? This is my house now. You have no right to be here." His smile dazzled her, as it had in years past and his deep voice penetrated her very soul. How she missed his arms around her, his gentle kiss. Everything about the way he was in the beginning.

"Baby, I want to talk to you. Please, let me in."

Baby, he hadn't called her that since months before the divorce was final. "Go back to town, get a motel and sleep it off."

"I don't need to sleep anything off, Jude. I'm sober, I swear."

The same old lie. Would he ever give up? "If you're sober why'd you run into something on the main road trying to pull in?"

"Helloooo...There's two feet of snow on the ground and the grader hasn't been by." He leaned against the door frame. "Once I lost you, Jude, I knew I'd thrown away the best thing that ever happened to me. I wanted to make sure I could stay sober before I tried to get you back. Baby, I've been sober for almost a year now."

She didn't want to listen, but he was saying everything she'd dreamed of hearing since they'd separated. "How can I believe you?"

"Let me in, smell my breath. I promise. It's true. I even got my job back. They gave me a leave of absence for six weeks. I told them how much I love you and that I had to have you back."

Did she dare trust him? Her mind screamed no, but her heart cried yes. Yes! Cautiously she reached for the lock, released it and stood back while Charlie greeted the man he'd known all of his life.

When Zach met her gaze, she almost lost her breath. He looked wonderful. Strong, handsome and...sober. The warmth of his arms penetrated the heavy coat she wore and his breath was a whisper on her lips.

"See? No whiskey breath."

His mouth took hers in a passionate kiss and she melted into his embrace. She fought the urge to protest when he released her. His dark brown eyes were indeed clear and his mouth sweet with his unique taste.

"I'm sorry, sweetheart, for the heartache I've caused you. If you'll give me a second chance, I'll prove I can be the best husband you could ever want."

~ ~ ~ ~ ~

"Now this is what I'm talking about, Charlie." Judith smiled and let the sun warm her face as she edited the last page of her novel. "Springtime in the Ozarks, you can't beat it, old buddy." Zach's arms came around her from behind the porch swing. His warm breath made her shiver with delight when he whispered in her ear.

"You can't beat falling in love all over again either."

It was true. It had been a month since he'd crashed into the mailbox and shown up on her doorstep. One glorious springtime month filled with love, sobriety and writing.

THE LOOK OF FOREVER

The florescent lights in the old train depot flickered with an unsteady rhythm. It was close to midnight and only a few people milled about while Julia made her way to the attendant's desk. "Is the 203 running on time?" She watched the thin man with a drawn face glance up from his paperwork and look at a computer screen.

"Looks like it, ma'am."

"Thanks." She found a chair and took a seat, thankful she wouldn't have to wait too long. She had an eerie feeling. She couldn't put her finger on it, but something just wasn't right. Oh well, she knew it would pass when her husband arrived, hopefully, safely.

Her favorite past time was people watching, and what a perfect time to take advantage of something she loved. She glanced around the depot and someone caught her attention.

A young woman, with a small child in tow, approached a pay phone. Their hair was mussed, and it looked as if they hadn't slept in days. Her heart went out to them as she watched the lady dig in her pocket for, she assumed, a quarter. Soon the woman abandoned her search, took the child's hand and walked away from the phone. As they passed, she saw a silent tear spill from the young mother's eye.

Julia held up her hand to stop the woman. "Just a minute." She was thankful she had never been in that position, but, if she had, would someone have helped her? She reached into her bag, pulled out some money and gave it to the lady. For such a small amount of giving the hug she got from the little girl was more gratifying than any payback could have ever been.

After they said thank you and walked away, she averted her gaze, and encountered an older couple. The man was well built for his age and wore a closely cropped, flat top haircut. Dressed in a nice short-sleeved shirt and crisply pressed jeans, he appeared comfortable. The woman with him held an air of class. Her gray hair was done neatly atop her head, and she wore a red business suit with a gold shirt and matching gold shoes. They made an interesting pair, he more casual, she more sophisticated, but somehow they went together perfectly.

She continued to study the people around her, but none piqued her interest as much as the young woman and the older couple. She glanced up at the big faced clock on the wall. In only five minutes Keith's train would arrive.

He didn't like it when he had to leave her and the kids, and neither did she. His business called him away too much as far as she was concerned. Why, she was only twenty-seven, and sometimes she felt like she had no life other than providing happiness to her family. Guilt plagued her. She often wondered what she had missed in life, if anything. She'd been lucky to find such a hardworking man, but—

Out of the corner of her eye, something caught her attention. She turned her head and saw a man. A stranger. Or was he? He hadn't been there moments earlier. It seemed he'd materialized out of thin air.

Her mind was playing tricks on her. She glanced at her watch and realized it had been hours since she'd eaten. This feeling was strange, she didn't like it at all. Maybe she needed some water, or to sit down.

Once again her gaze focused on the man. Everything around her seemed to fade to black. Except him. The peculiar feeling she'd had earlier crept back into her heart, her soul. She felt alone, frightened, but why? Did she know this man? She couldn't see his face, only his profile.

He stood tall. His dark hair glistened in the artificial light. Power drifted from his broad shoulders, his jeans fit snugly, and the tailored shirt he wore clung to his muscular chest.

Barely above a whisper, an alien voice escaped her throat, "It can't be." Suddenly he turned and met her gaze. She thought her heart would stop its wild beating completely. "Oh, my God."

She saw a spark flicker in his dark brown eyes. The look he gave her made an ember smoldered then slowly ignited a flame deep within her memory. Billy Joe Riley? But he was . . .dead. He shot her a sideways grin that made her warm all over. There it was, the look he said she'd always see that let her know he'd love her forever. Was this a dream?

Goose flesh rose on her skin and a strange force pulled at her very being. Something wasn't right. She was being drawn by an entity she couldn't explain. A blue nothingness pulled her deeper and deeper into its depths. What was happening?

Her mind reeled. Her body spiraled downward into the indigo gloom. She swallowed the bitter bile that threatened to choke her as she swirled in the bottomless pit. She fought to bring herself back, but knew the battle was lost when numbness consumed her. Closing her eyes, she allowed the darkness to surround her while something akin to memories flooded her mind.

~ ~ ~ ~ ~

Julia had been home from school for only a few hours when a knock at the back door drew her from her homework. Her heart skipped, she knew who it was and went to answer. Billy Joe stood in the yellow light of the porch lamp. The affect he had on her was amazing and she said the words she knew could get her into trouble. "They're gone."

"Can I come in?"

She took him by the hand and led him inside to the dingy old couch in the living room of her stepfather's house. They shouldn't be doing this, but she snuggled deeper into Billy's embrace as they kissed. Their lips parted and Billy Joe's warm breath brushed her cheek.

"I love you, Julia."

Her gaze met his. "Yes. I can tell by the look in your eyes, Billy."

"Always look into my eyes if you have any doubt that I love you. They will tell you what's in my soul."

She studied him and memorized the look. Longing overwhelmed her. "Take me, Billy. My stepfather's out with his girlfriend for the night and my mom's at work. They won't be home for hours. I want you to make me yours forever."

"Are you positive, baby? I don't want to hurt you. We've never gone all the way, and once we start, I'm not sure I'll be able to stop."

Should she go to the limit? The love she felt at this moment would never be matched, she was sure of that. She reached up and turned off the lamp, leaving only the moonlight that streamed through the window to illuminate the room. When she spoke, her voice was low, and she was surprised at how husky it sounded. "Take me."

He answered her request with a passionate kiss. When he backed away, he gently unbuttoned the summer shirt she wore and let it fall open to expose her breasts. It made her feel free.

She thought she could actually see fire dancing in his eyes as his gaze devoured her. His hand trailed up her stomach, leaving behind a searing path that would come to an end at her bosom. Where had all these feelings been hidden?

The heat of his touch continued to pierce her skin as he tenderly caressed one of her breasts. When he bent his head and took its crown into his mouth, she shivered and a new sensation washed over her. Warmth engulfed her heart, and she knew their love would last a lifetime.

Standing, Billy leaned over her. She didn't protest when he removed her jeans and surveyed her form.

"You're beautiful, Julia. I've never seen a naked woman before. I didn't know it would be like this."

At that moment she truly felt like a woman. Even if she was only sixteen years old.

The pieces of his clothing dropped to the floor, and he stood in front of her fully exposed.

Flush rushed to her face, but she didn't look away. She wanted to remember this moment forever. Could there be anyone more perfect than him in the world?

He knelt beside the couch. "I love you."

She ran her fingers through his soft hair and paused at the back of his neck. "I love you, too." She pulled him to her and pressed her lips to his. Somehow, she'd never noticed that he smelled so ... so manly. Probing his mouth with her tongue, she tasted his uniqueness.

When their lips separated once again, he brought his tall frame off the floor and lay next to her. Their bare skin touched, and she felt his passion radiate through her.

She hesitantly reached down and touched him. "Billy, I don't know what's happening to me. I feel . . . I don't know, I feel different. Like I'm all grown up."

"Me too."

They touched, kissed and explored each other's

bodies. She could speak no louder than a whisper, "Billy."

She didn't have to say another word. Slowly, gently, he brought himself over her. Scared but not ashamed, she gave herself willingly.

In the aftermath of the most wonderful experience of her life, she lay in Billy Joe's arms. "I guess this means I'm really a woman now."

"I've always thought you were a woman."

The front door burst open. She heard a click and the overhead light came on. The dark rage of her stepfather's glare threatened to stop her heart.

"What the hell is going on here?"

Fear engulfed her and she clutched for something to cover herself with. "Bo!"

Billy Joe jumped up and quickly pulled on his pants.

Her stepfather's eyes narrowed. "Why you slut. You've been doing this punk, haven't you?" He lunged toward Billy. "I'll kill you, you little bastard."

She fumbled for her clothes. "No, wait!"

"Wait my ass!"

Horrified, she watched. When Bo reached Billy he jabbed a fist into the young man's stomach. She couldn't stop the scream that escaped her throat as her lover fell to the floor. "Don't! Bo, please!"

Billy scurried off the floor, ran over to the small wood stove in the corner of the room and picked up the poker. "Don't come near me."

The cynical laugh that came from deep within Bo's chest caused her blood to run cold. She'd heard that laugh before. Bo was a dangerous man.

"What are you going to do, Punk?"

"I . . . I don't know, but I mean it," Billy said, *"don't come near me."*

Julia thought her heart was going to jump out of her chest. Fully clothed, she went to Bo's side and grabbed his arm. "Leave him alone!"

Bo backhanded her across the room. "Shut up, whore. I'm going to show him what it's like to deal with a real man."

Rubbing her jaw, tears blurred her eyes, but she saw the fury that covered Billy Joe's face. He rasped out a warning.

"Don't you ever touch her again."

Bo walked over to where she had landed on the floor. "Who, her? And what are you going to do if I do this?" He kicked her hip with the toe of his boot.

Agony shot through her, and she squeezed her eyes shut. The wail of a madman reached her ears. Hard footsteps crossed the room, and she heard a dull thud. She opened her eyes to see Bo's limp body fall to the floor. Billy Joe stood over him, blood dripped from the poker he held in his hand.

Silence filled the room. Billy dropped the weapon and frantically gathered the rest of his clothes.

She stared in disbelief at the unconscious form of her stepfather. A faraway voice penetrated her shock.

"Julia?"

Looking up, she saw Billy standing in front of her. He took her hand and pulled her off the floor. Tears welled in his eyes.

"I couldn't stand to see him hurting you. I got so

mad, I lost it. I'm sorry but I think he's dead, I've gotta go."

She melted into his arms and he kissed her with the most intense emotion she'd ever faced. Their gazes locked. She saw into his soul just as he said she would. His look told her he'd love her forever and beyond.

As her true love ran out of the house, she heard her stepfather groan. She wanted Billy to get away, far away, before Bo came to; but it looked as if that wasn't going to be the case.

His eyelids fluttered open, and he glanced around the room. "Where is he?"

"He's gone, and you'll never find him."

"I'll hunt him down till I take my last breath, girl." He stood and grabbed the shotgun from the rack mounted on the wall. "You can bet on it."

She heard Bo cock the shotgun before he rushed out. She held her breath for what seemed like hours, but she knew only seconds had passed. A shotgun blast rang in her ears. Then another. "Noooo!"

Darkness overwhelmed her as she fell to the floor.

~ ~ ~ ~ ~

"Julia? Darling? Are you okay? You look like you've seen a ghost."

The tiled floor was cold and hard beneath her. "K--Keith? What happened?"

"You fainted, honey."

Fainted? A ghost? Billy. "Billy!" Why had the memory been so vivid?

"Who's Billy, sweetheart?"

"No one, I-I guess I was dreaming." She craned her neck until she met Billy Joe's gaze.

He was real. Wasn't he? But how could that be? The man was dead. He smiled brightly, and she recognized the words that formed on his lips before his image began to fade.

"I love you, Julia."

He loved her. She had adored him in her youth, but now she loved another. She realized she needed to tell him, but words wouldn't work. She spoke silently and with all of her inner strength, she willed him to know her feelings.

The message his eyes conveyed, told her he understood and accepted the fact that, though they wouldn't be together, he would hold a special place in her heart for eternity.

"Honey, are you okay?" Keith asked.

Just as he had appeared, Billy Joe Riley vanished. She felt peacefulness inside that had been missing for years.

Glancing up at her husband she assured him, "Fine, sweetheart. Let's go home."

ETERNITY WAITS

The pounding of horse hoofs reached his ears before the riders came into sight. Four men pointed their guns toward the sky. Jack Waters recognized each and every one of them, and next time he was in town, he would be sure to tell the sheriff of their shenanigans...again. It wasn't the first time Luther Wilcox's men tormented him and Lilly.

"Get off my land, you sons-a-bitches!" He started toward the house to get his weapon; but before he could move, shots echoed against the hills as the men fired into the air. The hooligans' laughter, whoops and hollers rang out as they rode away.

A soft whimper was barely audible through the fading noise. He glanced to where his wife stood. "No!" Jack's heart sank to the pits of hell as he watched the woman he loved fall to the ground. "Lilly!" He ran to her and sank to his knees. One of the bullets had fallen from the heavens and struck her.

Blood stained the ground beneath her. She was limp when he pulled her into his arms. "Lilly.

Lilly!" She didn't move. He needed to do something, but helplessness threatened to tear him apart. "You're going to be okay, my love. I'm gonna go get the doc."

He picked her up, carried her inside then lay her flaccid body on their bed. "I'll hurry." Her tortured moan tore at his soul. She stirred and he reached for her hand. She was alive. "Lilly?" When her eyes fluttered open they were filled with pain. Her voice was a mere whisper and he leaned down to hear her words.

"Don't...leave...me. It's...too...late."

Tears spilled freely down his face. What would he do without her? "You're not going to die." He heard an unnatural pleading in his own voice when his statement changed to a request and he sobbed. "Don't die, Lilly, please."

Blood trickled from her mouth. The sticky red substance marked her pillow. Why did this have to happen? Thoughts of the men who did this rushed through his mind. If his beloved died his life would mean nothing. He vowed to get revenge by law or by his own hand. Lilly's whisper tugged at his breaking heart.

"I...love...you...Jack."

"My God!" He wiped his tear-stained face with his sleeve. "I love you, too, Lil." He knelt by the bed, took her in his arms realizing he had only said those words a few times.

Heat ebbed from her body, her life was fading away. He couldn't leave her to go and get the doctor. Not when she was on her way to heaven. With his darling in his embrace, he took a seat on the bed, leaned back onto the rough wood headboard and held her until she took her last breath.

Alone, the only sound was his own breathing. She was gone. His heart shattered into a million pieces and the scream that ripped from his chest was its own entity. When he caught his breath, he lay Lilly's lifeless body onto the mattress and covered her with a quilt she'd made with her own hands. "I'll join you soon, Lil."

Nothing in life had prepared him for the emotions he felt at that moment. He took his wife's well-worn Bible from the table beside the bed, then left the small room and made his way to the hearth. The shotgun was cool to the touch when he pulled it from the mantel.

Even if he died today, justice would be served. Those men would pay one way or the other. However, he couldn't bear the thought of his sweet wife not getting a proper burial. He placed the Holy Book, shotgun, and some extra cartridges on the kitchen table then made his way to the barn for the shovel.

~ ~ ~ ~ ~

It was time to ride. Jack made sure the Bible was in the saddle bag and the shotgun in its sheath before he mounted. He felt in his shirt pocket, several shells were there. Satisfied everything was in place, he took one last look around his little farm.

"Nothing." He patted his horse on the neck. "This place means nothing to me now."

His heart hurt. It felt like a stone, heavy in his

chest as he glanced at the makeshift cross he'd placed on his Lilly's grave. One of her favorite things to do was going onto the knoll beneath the trees to have a picnic. He'd always acted like he didn't want any part of it, but she always saw right through him and they'd end up sitting on the ground enjoying the time together.

Things that happened on that hill, their special spot, would remain cherished memories. Now the mound would be her forever resting place. God, how he missed her laughter, her loving smile and her soft hands touching his skin.

"Bastards!" He heeled his horse into a gallop. Once he explained to Sheriff Mansel what had happened, the killers would get what they had coming to them. He hoped to see them strung up and swinging from the tallest tree in town.

His spurs jingled with each step as he made his way along the wooden sidewalk to the sheriff's office. He opened the door then stepped inside. Cigar smoke was thick and the potbellied Wayne Mansel sat behind his desk.

"What can I do for you, Waters?"

"Wilcox's men came to the ranch this morning."

The sheriff sat back in his chair. "And?"

"They killed my Lilly. I want you to put 'em behind bars."

Mansel sat forward once again. "How'd it happen, Jack?"

"There were four of them. They came up toward the house and before I could get my gun they started shooting into the air. One of the bullets came down and hit my wife." He took off his hat and, trying to calm himself, he turned it in his hands. He looked the other man in the eye. "They're killers, Wayne. Plain and simple they need to pay."

Shaking his head Mansel said, "Now I can't go off half-cocked and arrest four men. Especially when none of them actually pointed their gun at Lilly and pulled the trigger. I'm sorry she's gone, I know you loved her; but, Jack, it was an accident."

Jack put his hat on and noticed his hands trembled. His blood boiled and his heart pained as it pumped the hot liquid through his veins at an accelerated rate. "It's not right! I'll have no more of it!" He turned his back to the sorry excuse of a lawman and started toward the door.

"Stop right there, Waters. If you go after them, you'll be the murderer and *I'll* have to come after *you*."

He paused, straightened his back then opened the door. "I'll be seein' you, Mansel." He slammed the door behind him, got on his horse and rode west toward the Wilcox ranch."

All he could see was the crimson fluid of his Lilly's life seeping from her body. Red, that's the color that shrouded his soul. Red for anger, red for the torment his heart was in, but most of all, red for the hatred he felt toward the bastards that turned his world upside down and sent Lilly to meet her Maker way too soon.

He reached into his saddle bag and pulled out the Good Book Lilly had held in her sweet hands so many times. Raising it to his lips he prayed. "Heavenly Father, I'm gonna ask Your forgiveness for what I'm about to do. I reckon You already know what it is, so I don't have to tell Ya. If I don't get to heaven because of my sins, I ask that You take good care of my Lilly. Thank You, Sir." He kissed the book and put it back in its place.

Smoke? He smelled smoke. He glanced up and saw the beginnings of a plume rise above the trees in the west. It was Wilcox's place. "Damn, is the place on fire?"

Urging his horse into a gallop, he hastened toward the growing cloud of black. Then the crackling sound of the flames came to his ears along with a woman's cry. What the hell was going on?

He rounded the corner to see what was on fire. It was the bunk house. The woman was Mrs. Wilcox. She was trying to go inside. Jack reined his horse to a stop, jumped off then ran toward her and the burning building. Tears fell onto her cheeks and her voice was strained when she spoke.

"Help me, please!"

From the looks of the flames, it was too late to save the building. If anyone was inside, it was probably too late for them, too. "Back away, ma'am. There's nothing we can do."

She grabbed Jack's arm. "But Bob's in there. He went in to wake up the hands and never came out. We need to save him."

He thought of the drunken men that had killed Lilly. They must have come back here and passed out. No telling how the fire started. Mrs. Wilcox's face showed her fear when she spoke to him. His heart went out to her.

"My husband's all I have."

Her husband? His Lilly was all he'd had and he

knew what this lady was going through. As if the hand of God propelled him forward, he ran through the black smoke that billowed out the doorway then fell to the floor and began to crawl. His heart pounded hard in his chest. "Hello, can you hear me?" He listened, nothing. "Is anyone here?"

"Over here."

The voice was strong, yet weak at the same time. He couldn't really tell where it had come from. The heat was so intense it felt like the flames licked at his back. He started to turn back then thought of the grieving woman outside. "Say again!"

"Over here!"

This time he got a fix on the voice and crawled toward it. The noise was deafening and a crash sounded as one of the walls collapsed. One side of the ceiling fell, barely missing him. Pain riddled his chest and back. Had he been hit by something? No matter, he had to hurry or the inferno would be the death of both of them.

His lungs burned and for the second time that day the smell of death reached his nostrils. He hoped the ceiling hadn't crashed on top of the man. "Wilcox, you still with me?"

"Yes, here."

The voice was close. Jack reached out his hand and felt the man's leg. He was sitting on the floor leaned against the side wall of the building. Fire was quickly engulfing everything, and the pain in Jack's chest wouldn't let up. Squeezing, it felt like it was pushing the air right out of his lungs, then he realized it was all the smoke he was breathing in. "Can you walk?"

"No. I stumbled running in and I think I broke my leg."

It took all of Jack's strength to stand, but he managed to grab the older man under the arms. Everything moved in slow motion as he desperately made his way to the door. The hands of time seemed to stand still, but finally he saw the light of day as he pulled Wilcox out and away from the blazing ruins.

Mrs. Wilcox fell to her knees beside her husband. "Oh, Bob, I was so scared. Are you okay?"

"Broke my leg, Mary, but I'm fine."

Jack lay on the ground. He couldn't breathe and the pain in his back and chest was worse than ever. What was happening to him? He heard the sound of horses approach.

Mr. Wilcox spoke. "It's the sheriff."

Mansel dismounted. "Did Waters do this?"

"No, I don't even know what he's doing here."

"Lilly was killed this morning by a stray bullet one of your hands fired."

"Aw, hell."

Mrs. Wilcox said, "He saved Bob's life. If he hadn't shown up when he did, I'd be a widow, Sheriff.

Mansel pointed to Jack. "What's wrong with him, was he burned in the fire or something?"

"I don't know. The ceiling collapsed, maybe something hit him."

The sheriff knelt down. "Don't see no blood. He sure has a funny grey color about him, though."

Their voices faded and Jack tried to focus on

what was in front of him. What was it? Who was it? Lilly? The most beautiful sight met Jack's gaze. Lilly stood in front of a rainbow of bright light. Colors he'd never seen before illuminated behind her. They encircled her and she was more radiant than she'd ever been. She glowed with happiness and love.

The cold he'd felt only moments ago disappeared and warmth overtook him. The most beautiful music seemed to lift him up. It sounded like angels singing. His pain was gone and he stood to meet his wife's gaze. "Is this –" Though she didn't speak, somehow her voice rang clear.

"Heaven." Lilly smiled joyfully and held out her hand. He knew eternity waited.

JANET KAY GALLAGHER

＊▶▶◀◀＊

Janet Kay Gallagher is a Christian Author. Both my parents were readers, and my earliest memories are filled with fun trips to the library. My parents read the BIBLE and the CHILDREN'S CLASSIC STORIES to my brother Bob and I before bed. In the days before television, the newspaper and radio were our news and entertainment. Sunday morning, we ran out and got the newspaper and jumped in bed with Dad and Mom, and Dad read the comics to us. Like some of our favorites, TERRY AND THE PIRATES, DICK TRACY, LIL'ABNER, and DAGWOOD AND BLONDIE. Later in the day he would read items from the newspaper about trees and planets and anything of interest.

Two librarians had a positive impact on my reading. Mrs. Warren made sure I was reading the books in my age group, she knew if I had checked them out to read. I was impressed by the personal care and guidance of Mrs. Warren.

I loved Mrs. Tierney's Seventh Grade Library Training Class. Checking out books and working in the school library was fun. Mrs. Tierney gave personal attention to the books I read and discussed them with me.

I enjoyed reading to my two boys Stephen and Ken. When Stephen was in fourth grade I was told he had Dyslexia. That explained my own reading problems. And why the librarians helping keep my reading up to my grade levels meant so much to me. When I was in school it didn't have a name. Mom couldn't understand why I couldn't tell the difference in, The and the, since they were the same word.

I still read daily or listen to books read by my Kindle Fire. I'm also a big fan of Audiobooks.

Now I'm writing short stories and poems and my own books. I hope my readers will enjoy them and remember the stories.

THE LAST DAY ON EARTH

I want to go out of this life praising GOD
I want my family and friends to know I love them
I want to be known as an encourager
I want to be remembered for laughing and enjoying
the life God gave me

I hope my family will be happy I was part of their
lives
I hope my friends are glad they knew me
I hope others will be glad I lived
I hope my books will continue to be read

I am happy to be living, loving, and enjoying Gods
gifts
I love the beauty I see, flowers and trees and
changing seasons
I see the beauty and goodness in the people around
me
I pray my last day on earth will end with Jesus
welcoming me home

CHANGE OF FORTUNE

Paula opened her large fortune Cookie. The paper said, "Your life is in danger. Say nothing to anyone. You must leave the city immediately and never return. Repeat: Say nothing..."

Paula told her date, "Mark, I'll be right back, I'm headed to the ladies room." She picked up her purse and left the table. *It's a good thing I always take my purse. I never trusted Mark Stanton enough to leave it at the table. Where has that thought come from? I never realized*

that is why I take my purse with me.

At the restroom door she checked to find out if Mark could see her. He was half turned with his back to her, talking to someone at another table. Good, she went past the ladies room and into the kitchen.

Her favorite waiter, Chen saw her, and came to ask, "Did you need something Miss Paula?"

"Chen, I'm leaving. Can you cover for me and not let on that you saw me go out?" she asked.

"Miss Paula, I won't say anything, and no one else will. Glad you read the fortune cookie.

That is why I waited to bring them when your young man was in the restroom. May you find peace and happiness. Go far away."

It wasn't until she was on the highway that she began to wonder why and how Chen would know she was in danger. Did he know something about Mark's past? Was Mark putting out some kind of dangerous vibe that people were picking up on? Maybe she was being foolish. But she had felt frightened for a while. Mark had become bossy and possessive and insisted on them getting married right away. She put him off by saying she wanted a big wedding and she wouldn't elope as he wanted. And that it took time to plan a wedding.

Paula didn't love Mark and couldn't marry him. Tonight, she was leaving town, all her belongings were packed into her Durango this afternoon before going to the China Bowl Restaurant to meet him. She had planned to tell him she was moving but kept putting it off all through dinner.

Her landlord had received notice a month in advance and a couple of days ago he told her the apartment had been leased.

She realized she wasn't in love but was afraid to tell Mark. What was it that she feared? She had seen him in a rage once when a man said something quietly to him. And he had been mean and possessive when a man she worked with spoke to her when they were out on a movie date. Afterward she thought Mark's third degree would go on forever. Another time he had grabbed her wrist when he got mad at her over something trivial. It was like a vise and it tightened enough for her to feel real pain. She thought he was going to break her wrist. She screamed and her neighbor Brandon opened her door and asked, phone in hand, "Do I need to call the police?"

Yes, all those things were building to the danger point in her mind. She was really escaping from Mark. That was what all of this is about. Why didn't it show up in her vision as menacing before now? It was easy to imagine Mark becoming a wife beater, or he might have killed her as suggested in the Fortune Cookie.

Paula moved to a picturesque town outside Boston. She got her license and sold Real Estate and was happy for several years. Until today when she boarded the Boston to New York Commuter Train. She was still in the aisle when she spotted Mark. She edged down the aisle and went to the next door and got back off the train just before the doors closed and it pulled out. Mark looked out the window and their eyes met. She got to her car crying and trembling. She knew it would be an hour before Mark could get off the train and start back taking another hour. She had to move fast two hours wasn't much time. As she drove she told her phone to call her husband William Barton.

"William, thank God you answered right away. Mark has found me. He got on the train and when I saw him, I was able to get off before the doors closed. Our eyes met. I'm so scared. I think it will be a couple of hours before he could get back here."

"Come to my office. Tim Marshall just came in and we'll protect you. That's why you married a private detective isn't it?" He joked.

"Very funny most of the time but not right now. I'm relieved and on my way to you."

When she arrived, William came out to the car and walked her into the office and hugged her until she stopped shaking. "I told Tim about Mark. Take a look at the profile information I have now. Don't worry we'll keep you safe. After all you're my wife and my life." He said.

Tim said, "It must have been a shock to find out all this police information about someone you were going out with. Good thing you left when you did. Read over the report. Then tell us anything you can remember from this scare today. Describe what he was wearing." He handed her the report.

She read the details and shuddered. "It has been a long time since I last read this. It seems worse than I remembered. I don't know how I could have missed being on the receiving end of the violence he put others through. Today his hair was a bit shorter and had a little amount of gray at the temples. When our eyes met he looked totally evil. That is the only word I can think of for that look. Do you two ever get so frightened you feel like you can't move? I hope not because it could be hazardous in your line of work. That is how I felt. But I was able to move quickly because I had to get away."

William said, "You did the best thing you could have done. I wonder if he followed you to the Rail Station, or if he didn't know you were here until he saw you? If he knew he will be following soon if not it will take awhile for him to locate you. And learn your new name. I'll call Benson at the police station and get our information on him updated. I haven't even thought about Mark Stanton for a long time."

Tim said, "I just looked up your Amtrack train and it only had six stops before it arrives at the station in New York. Paula you are probably correct about the two-hour time for Mark to return but it could be less.

Paula called her office. "Hi Mr. Huston, I need to take off some personal time. My last sale closed on Monday. Karen has my appointment calendar and can assign someone to cover them for me. And I'd appreciate one of the other realtors handling anything that comes in for me while I'm out of the office. I'm not sure how long it will take. I hope this works out for you." She waited to see what he would say.

"Paula, I hope all is well with you. You aren't sick are you?" he said.

"No, I'm fine just need some time off. Is that ok with you?"

"Sure. You're my favorite salesperson. Please don't tell the others I said that. Come back as soon as you can."

"I won't tell because I know you tell each of us that we are your favorite. I'll be returning as soon as I can. Bye now." She said and hung up.

William hung up his phone and said. "Benson gave me more information. Mark was arrested about six months after you left San Francisco. And spent five years in prison. He was arrested four years after he got out for spousal abuse and attempted murder. The woman nearly died. Mark has been free for almost two years and doesn't have any arrests during that time. I hate the fact that he knows you're here."

Paula started laughing. "I'm glad he didn't get arrested until after I left. I'd have never met you, and would probably still be in San Francisco. That fortune cookie got me away from a bad man, and brought me here to find the perfect husband."

William and Tim and Paula were on constant alert mode for days before anything happened. They were tired and wanted to stop the drama of watching and listening for every footstep or sounds or looking for shadows.

William and Paula woke up when the picture window downstairs in the living room shattered. They grabbed robes and started down the stairs where they found Tim using the fire extinguisher on the curtains. A big rock had broken the window and two Molotov Cocktails came in after it.

When Tim got the fire out he said, "Well I guess the war with Mark has started."

William called Detective Benson and he came and took a report. A friend fixed the big window.

Tim bought a couple more fire extinguishers and put up a couple perimeter alarms. They decided to stay at the house and meet the attacks there. While he was out he had brought more food from Paula's list.

Paula spent the day cooking. She made a large pot of spaghetti and meatballs. A roast with potatoes and onions and two meatloaves. When they cooled she froze most of the food. It had been a productive day.

The next attack was also fire. Started on the outside of the house with several big piles of wadded up newspapers that were set on fire against the sides of the house. But it didn't catch the house. Tim and William went to put them out.

William said, "I was afraid he would start one outside so each night I have been watering the house and the wooden porch. Stay here we'll be right back."

"I wondered why you spent all that time outside each night. Be safe." Paula said.

She heard the kitchen glass break. Picked up her gun from the table next to her chair and went to the kitchen just as Mark stepped in the back door.

"Well, look at you with a gun, shaking and too scared to use it. You're still as pretty as ever. Paula you know I loved you and we were going to be married. Why did you tease me that way? Why did you run away? When I got to your apartment the landlord told me you moved out. And he didn't know where you had gone. That nosey neighbor came out into the hall with his phone again, and said he'd already called the police." Mark said.

She stood there looking at him, still pointing the gun.

He continued, "I've had a terrible life because of you. And you married this William guy and have a beautiful house and new cars and fancy clothes. You were supposed to be mine for life. But you left me alone. I always knew I would find you. It's taken years and lots of money to locate you. I'm giving you a second chance. Come with me right now and we will get married and spend our life together as we promised all those years ago." He started to move toward her.

"Stop where you are. I'm married and won't go anywhere with you. I know how to shoot this gun so stay back." Paula pulled her phone out of her pocket and dialed 9-1-1. The operator said, "9-1-1 how may I help you?"

Mark said, "I didn't want to kill you but you made your choice." A knife was in the hand that had been behind him. He moved toward her. Paula shot him. He dropped the knife and blood flowed down his arm. Mark ran out the back door.

William and Tim had the fires out.

Paula ran out of the house after Mark and yelled at William, "Stop him."

William and Tim gave chase but Mark reached his car and sped off and ran into the patrol car that was turning into their street.

Tim said, "I'll handle Mark you check the cops"

William found the officers weren't badly hurt and one of them had called for back-up and an ambulance.

William called Detective Benson who met them at the hospital Emergency Room. The police officers were checked out and released. They took the information for their reports and left the hospital.

Mark Stanton was in surgery. He had lost a lot of blood from the gunshot wound that did a great deal of damage to his right arm. The Doctor wasn't sure if they could save the arm or not. From the car crash he had broken his left ankle and also a broken bone above the knee on that leg and had internal injuries. He had a concussion and lots of scratches and bruises. As the nurses wheeled Mark down the corridor to surgery, he saw Paula and started shouting over and over. "Paula I'm going to kill you."

Detective Phillip Benson had already arrested Mark and assigned officers to guard him when he gets out of surgery. He had recorded Marks ravings threatening to kill Paula. And gone to the house and had it gone over as an active crime scene. And taken Mark's knife off the kitchen floor.

Benson said. "With all the evidence we have collected we can put Mark Stanton away for a long time. This will be his second trial for attempted murder. All of you did a great job."

"Thanks. How about you and your wife Alva coming to dinner next Saturday. At 7 P.M." Paula said.

"You know Alva and I will want to hear the whole story from you." Benson said.

San Francisco Today

At the China Bowl restaurant, the waiter Chen assured Miss Marion that, "I won't tell anyone I saw you leave and neither will the rest of the staff."

She moved quickly out the back door.

Yan laughed "I wonder how many women have left like that over the years? How do you think your warnings affect their lives. Do they actually leave town? They always look so scared. For a long time now I've been expecting the boss to catch on about your special fortune cookies, and fire you."

Chen smiled with glee then said, "Don't worry. Many of the women pay no attention to the fortune cookie. If they run, it's because they don't trust the person they're with at the time. I always wait until the boss is away before giving them out. It's just a fun harmless game I play."

GONE

One moment you are talking to me
You slump in the chair next to me
That quick you are gone
After almost thirty years you leave me

Slowly I've learned how to go on
You are still with me
When I look at the rug I get mad at you
Thinking of your treatment and love for my boys

I smile and thank you
So many little things, many unnoticed
Make up our feelings and heart
I am glad you were part of my life
You still influence my choices as I continue here
I plan to see you one day on God's side of life

PBX SWITCHBOARD OPERATOR

Answering Service and Physicians Exchange

"Dammit!" The minute I said it the room became pin drop quiet. It took five or six long strides for my boss Wayne to plug into my PBX Switchboard. He listened to my customers' cussing tirade a minute then said.

"John this is Wayne I am having my operator connect you to my office phone and we'll talk." He went back to his office and picked up his phone. I had it already connected.

The five of us operators, could hear Wayne's side of the conversation plain as day.

"John, you and I have been friends and you have been on the Answering Service for many years. But I can't allow my operators to be spoken to like you were doing just now. The young girl you were speaking to has never said anything back to a customer. She is a very good worker. I have warned you before to speak to them with respect. As of now you are no longer on our boards."

There was a pause while he listened. Then he said. "I don't know about our friendship, we will have to see about it. But I must protect my girls, so your service is disconnected as of now. Good-By."

It felt like everyone in the room was holding our breath to see if I would get fired.

Wayne came behind me again and plugged a peg into John Kearney Attorney at Law, office jack. Then he asked me to come into his office. I felt a little better when he didn't close the door. Maybe he just wanted to make an example to the others of what happens when you say something you shouldn't to a customer.

"I am so sorry." I blurted out before he could say anything.

"Don't worry. I knew I would have to do that to John one day. He has caused problems before and I have let him stay. Today was the last straw with me. Kay, you are a good operator. That is why you are on the old concentrator switchboard. When you are working it, we have less dropped calls and I haven't had to call the servicemen as often. You have a knack for toggling the keys. I know sometimes you need to listen to keep from losing a connection. I also know the client doesn't know you are on with them. That is fine just remember the confidentiality form you signed not to tell anything you hear. Take a break and go back to work."

"Thank You. I thought you would fire me for talking back to him and saying what I did."

"Don't do it again and we will be fine."

I went to the Kitchen and poured a cup of coffee. And let the tears flow. Jean came in and hugged me and told me it was ok, just the down feeling we have after high tension. Wayne is an easy boss to work for. I washed my face and went back to my switchboard and finished my shift. Tomorrow we would do it again.

I watched as the 5 pm shift came on. The doctor's offices were calling on the trunk lines to turn the office over to us for the night. They would tell us who was on call. Business' also logging out. The Alarm Company letting us know who was on call and offices turning their alarms over to us. Position one on the board handled the special alarm board and her switchboard number one. Board two had most of our doctors. Three was my concentrator switchboard. It was the oldest and would be replaced when the owners had enough money to do it. Board four and five had fewer customers and mostly businesses.

Above the connector lines we had shelves with cubby holes to hold our customer cards, where we wrote everything down and the time we got that information. Then the next operator, who had a person on that line knew exactly who was on call and how to handle the caller.

I enjoyed talking to all these people and handling their problems. Today I was glad to still have a job and tomorrow would start by having the offices check in, so we could give the lines back to them until noon check out.

On the way home I stopped for the Mexican combo-plate at Mama Lupe's. While I was having an iced tea, and waiting for the order, I sat at the picnic table. A policeman came over and spoke.

"Aren't you Kay McNabb, Bob's sister?"

"Yes, but do I know you?"

"I'm Clint Mathews. Our house was across the

alley from you when you lived on Jefferson."

"Oh, my. How did you end up as a policeman? I seem to remember the police bringing you home or picking you up at your house." What an awful thing to say. I could feel my face turning red.

"You're correct that was me. One of the officers convinced me that I needed to change and get on their side. He told me I could either be the one being put in jail or be the one putting others in jail. So, I straightened out and became a policeman about five years ago. I love being on the side of right."

"Wonderful news. My mom will be glad to hear about this. Bob is in Missouri and wants to be a farmer. He has one little boy and a nice wife. Are you married?"

"I'm engaged. Bob always wanted to be a farmer. Your mom was so beautiful. You are too, are you married?"

"No, I'm not. No one of interest at this time."

"That's my order ready. I am glad to have run into you. Here is my card if you should ever need a policeman." He picked up his order and left.

I watched that tall blond rugged looking man walk away from me. Wow, I didn't remember him looking that good when I was growing up, but then I was only starting in junior high.

Sunday after church I went to lunch at Maria's Restaurant with a high school friend Velma Warner. This place, our favorite, looks like a Mexican Inn. The flowers are beautiful, and the food is excellent.

"Do you remember Tall Paul Ambrose from Junior High?"

"You mean tall, dark and handsome Paul? Of course, too bad he was dealing drugs. He's been in and out of jail since high school. What a waste all those good looks and no brains. I heard somewhere that his uncle was connected, and Paul wanted to follow him. Kay, why did you ask me about him?"

"If he was dealing drugs back in junior high, why didn't I know about it?"

The waitress brought our lunch and refilled our coffee. After she walked away Velma answered.

"You were one of the good girls. Always talking about God and inviting everyone to church meetings. No one told you anything. When you walked by didn't you notice the boys stopped cussing, telling jokes. You were surrounded by a protective force. No one wanted to turn you from your life but didn't let you in on the seamy goings on."

"I didn't know. I asked about Paul because I talk to him every now and then in my job."

After leaving Velma I thought about the protection around me. It feels good to be considered one of the good guys. That must be how Clint feels about becoming a policeman. I couldn't tell Velma that we aren't able to call a Doctor for Paul because he's on our doctors drug list. All we can do is tell him to go to the emergency room for help.

I'm twenty-three and still wearing my hair in a ponytail or page boy. I need a new hairdo. These styles are easy to wear the headset at my job. I like the handset with the shoulder rest the best. Better get to work. The new minimum wage law of $1.25 is going into effect soon but it won't affect me since

I started at $1.30 an hour and after a year will get raised to $1.35. Hope the gas prices don't go up too much like everyone expects, .29.9 cents a gallon is high enough.

Mondays are always busy. My customers had checked in for the day and checked out for lunch. Most of them had checked back in for the afternoon when I answered Dr. Morris' office line. I couldn't hear anyone but knew from the raspy sound someone was there and needed help.

I calmly told the caller, "Dr. Morris' office girl will be back very soon. Please stay on the line with me and we will connect you to the doctor as soon as we can."

I closed my key and asked Jean, sitting next to me working the, all doctors board, to call Dr. Morris' back-office line and see if they could pick up. Sometimes they stayed in the office for lunch and just had us answer the phones. Before she had a chance to do what I asked, Dr. Morris called on her trunk line.

He told Jean to tell me to continue talking calmly to the patient. He could hear me and her, but we couldn't hear him. This was a problem with my concentrator board. I was given the message for her and passed it along.

"Mary, stay calm, the doctor is on the line with us. We can't hear him because of a problem with my equipment. He told me what to tell you. He has sent the paramedics to your house and he will meet you when you arrive at the hospital. Stay on the line with me until the help arrives at your home." I continued talking calmly to her.

The noises from Mary were sounding weaker. I kept talking. Goose bumps are rising on my arms.

"Mary, that sounds like a siren. Stay calm so they can help you." A couple of minutes later a man came on the phone and told me, "This is Officer Burns, the EMS team are working with Mary and will transport her to the hospital as soon as possible."

"Thank you, Officer, Doctor Morris will meet you at the hospital." I was able to disconnect.

Later that afternoon Dr. Morris called and asked to speak to our boss. After the conversation Wayne came and stood behind me and told me. "Kay, Dr. Morris was very impressed with how you recognized Mary had a serious problem and kept her on the line and calmed her down. She has Elephantiasis and it swells her up where she can't speak. When she gets excited it worsens her condition. By your calmness he had a better outcome with her this time."

Wow, a few days ago I lost us a customer and today got a commendation.

My days as a **PBX SWITCHBOARD OPERATOR** were exciting, stressful, scary, and rewarding. It was gratifying to know I helped people with their everyday needs and emergencies. Writing this brought back the goose bumps and fear I had felt while dealing with Mary all those many years ago. At the time this was going on (early 1960s) not everyone had a home phone, at that time they all were connected to the wall. In an emergency you went to the nearest neighbor who had a phone and asked to use it. Doctors used pagers, a few had mobile phones in their cars. Some of the business people used pagers too.

A few days ago, someone asked me what PBX stood for, it is Private Branch Exchange. A PBX Switchboard was a phone company connector board where the Answering Service Operator made connections for all calls going in and out of the office after hours. The trunk lines were the main lines coming into the answering service. Mrs. Olsen on Little House on the Prairie Series put one in her Hotel that looked, almost like the one I used. Sometimes you will see one in an old movie.

While working at this job I was the first one to hear the news. One of my customers called in and told me, "The Presidents been shot in Dallas." I turned around in my chair and told Wayne Burback, my boss. "Turn on the radio President Kennedy's been shot."

Not everyone had a television. At that time, it was only black and white. And only a few channels available. The President Kennedy story was on a continuous loop for days.

Several years later I worked at Beverly Hills Medical and Answering Service. I got to wake up the Bionic Woman. And was there during the Watergate Scandal. Spoke to many interesting people.

There was a drastic change in the look and working of the equipment a few years later and our old PBX Switchboards became obsolete. Offices now had a small unit on their desk about the size of our computer keyboard where a receptionist could direct calls with the push of a switch. No bulkier heavy switchboards with cords.

(Author's Note: This is a true story. I was proud of my work.)

YOUNG SLEUTHS

S ince school was out for the summer Marion and her friend Jimmy played detectives and had gotten good at following people without them noticing. Today at Annabelle's Drug Store they finished their cherry coke at the lunch counter.

Marion said, "I want to look for a book." She and Jimmy went to the book and magazine racks and saw a man wearing a monocle.

Jimmy nudged Marion with his elbow and whispered. "We have to follow him. He looks dangerous and interesting. Maybe he's a spy or something."

"You're right we must see where he goes. He looks familiar. Where would we have seen him?"

They watched out the window as he went out and crossed the street. They were on his trail. And made sure not to get too close. They kept other pedestrians between him and themselves. The man was window shopping and stopped at several locations but didn't go inside. About seven blocks from their start, he bought a ticket at the booth outside the theater. They watched until he went inside and bought popcorn and a drink and gave the usher his ticket and moved out of sight.

Marion said, "He will be in there a couple of hours we might as well go home for the day."

On the way home, Jimmy said, "I've got it. He looks like the Colonel Mustard card in our clue game!"

"Yes, you're right, I knew he looked like someone we should know." Marion said.

Jimmy said, "I'll bring my Colonel Mustard Card tomorrow. Maybe we'll see him again and can follow his movements.

The next day they walked around the downtown streets and spotted him going into the Woolworth's Store. He sat at the counter. They watched as he ordered and when he came out they followed him. First to the 3rd Street Pawn Shop. They couldn't see what he was doing inside. Then he went to Kay's Jewelers and spoke to a salesclerk. Next, he went to the Maywood Hotel. He spoke to the clerk at the desk and was handed mail and a newspaper. He sat beside a window and started to read.

Jimmy said, "He must live here. Let's go home and see if we can follow him tomorrow."

The next day they got to the Maywood Hotel in time to see Colonel Mustard going out. They followed him several more places and back to his home.

After almost a week following their suspect. Marion said, "It's a good thing we got these pocket notebooks like we saw Joe Friday and his partner use on Dragnet. We have kept track of the time we first spot him and each stop he makes. A pattern is clear. He follows his routine for each day."

Jimmy said, "When he leaves his hotel he goes to lunch at one of the lunch counters, then one of the pawn shops, then a jewelry store, and back to the hotel. On Wednesdays he changes and does lunch then a movie. On Monday and Friday his first stop is the Wells Fargo Bank, he goes to the lockbox area, then lunch and follows the rest of that days routine."

When they finished checking their lists of the Colonels activities they tried to figure out why he went to the pawn shops and the jewelry stores.

"Since we have been following Colonel Mustard so long we will have to be extra careful that he doesn't see us. What do you think he's up to with all the pawn shops and the jewelry stores?" Marion said.

Jimmy said, "Do you think he's buying from the pawn shop and getting it appraised at the jewelers? Maybe he's a thief selling to the pawn shops. Or maybe the pawn shops are fencing his goods?"

"If he is a thief, he'd store the newly stolen items in the bank. After they cooled down, he might take the items to the jeweler to be appraised. That way he would know what price to insist on from the pawn shop owners when he sold them." Marion said.

The next day, Marion spotted her friend Jimmy, by his bright red shaggy hair. He moved toward her as she waited by the Ice Cream Parlor. He was late because he had to go with his mother to an appointment. She was glad he found her. Following was more fun with two of them on the case."

Half a block away Colonel Mustard a

distinguished looking man entered the circular door of the Maywood Hotel.

Jimmy met her and they crossed the street to the Hotel. And peeked in the window as usual.

Colonel Mustard was sitting straight backed in a chair, they saw his white knuckles gripping the chair arm, another man sat opposite him. The stranger had blond hair. He looked scary. The man was big and his angry face pinched up in mean lines as he talked. Marion and Jimmy couldn't hear what they said. The men got up and went to the elevator. The children watched as the indicator hand moved and stopped on the seventh floor. The elevator stayed there.

"Now what, Marion?"

"It's almost dinnertime and our mothers will be looking for us. I wonder what the colonel and the other man argued about? The blond man must have already been here, we didn't see him go inside. We did good today. I'm sure we weren't noticed."

They walked back home. Marion said, "See you tomorrow, same time. We'll follow the Colonel again. Bye."

His eyes crinkled when he grinned and said, "See You."

When Marion arrived at the corner the next day, she glanced at the headlines in the newspaper box. "MAN KILLED IN MAYWOOD HOTEL KITCHEN." Her stomach quelled up. Her hand trembled as she dropped in the coins. She sat down on the raised planter box surrounding a tree, to read the paper as dread tightened her throat. "MAYWOOD HOTEL" jumped off the page and her heart pounded faster. She read. "The morning cook found the body of an unidentified man. He had been shot. No one remembers seeing him in the hotel. No other information is available. The police would like any leads. Do You know this man? See the Police sketch below." The small sketch on the page asking for information to identify the murdered man, showed the blond man they had seen yesterday with Colonel Mustard in the Maywood Hotel lobby.

Marion let out a startled yelp when Jimmy slid into the seat next to her.

"Look." She handed him the paper. "It's the mean looking guy that was with Colonel Mustard. Do you think he killed this man? We should tell the police what we know." They walked several blocks to the police station. Then hesitated to go inside.

"Jimmy, stand up as tall as you can, we have important evidence to give them."

Head high, backs straight they entered the building. The desk was old and over their heads. Marion patted her hand on top and got the attention of an officer.

He looked over the top and asked, "How can I help you?"

Marion cleared her throat and said, "We know something about the man that was shot in the Maywood Hotel."

He made a call and they were led to Detectives Jones, the tall thin one, and Detective Anders who had a kind face.

Jones said, "Please sit down and give us your names and addresses." When he had written down the information he said. "I'll be right back." He wasn't gone long and when he got back he said, "Tell us what you know about our case."

Anders noticed how fidgety the kids were and said, "It's okay to be nervous, tell us why you came here."

Jimmy nudged Marion.

She said, "I saw the newspaper headline and had a bad feeling. I bought it and read about the murder. The man in the picture is the blond, mean faced man we saw sitting in the hotel lobby yesterday about four-thirty P.M. He got into the elevator and it didn't stop until the seventh floor."

"Was he alone?" Anders asked.

The children shifted in their chairs, hating to tell about following the Colonel. The detectives watched and waited.

Jimmy burst out with, "Colonel Mustard was sitting with him."

Jones exploded. "Colonel Mustard!"

Marion pulled a card from her wallet. "The man we were following looked like our Colonel Mustard CLUE game card," she said.

"Why were you following him?" Jones asked.

"We spotted him and checked that card. We decided he was the one we should follow to hone our detective skills. Yesterday we followed him to the hotel. We looked in the window, they were sitting in the lobby, arguing. They didn't see us. When they went to the seventh floor, we went home. We have followed him two and a half weeks and have a list of his activities during the day." She handed him their log and the card.

Jones took the Clue card and the activity report, as it was labeled, to the Xerox machine. He came back and handed it to Marion. "Thank You for your information. You did the right thing coming to us. DO NOT FOLLOW anyone else. Is that understood? No more detecting. It could be dangerous. Your mothers are here to pick you up." he said.

After the children left, Detective Jones said, "That was a different addition to our day but it's a waste of time."

Detective Anders put the kids' log report down and laughed and said, "You didn't need to yell at them. I think they understood how dangerous it could have been. It was fun to hear their story. It may NOT have been a waste of time. As a matter of fact, I think they just handed us our killer. Look at her report of activities. He may be the burglar that has been so elusive. One of the residents at the hotel wears a monocle and could easily fit this game card picture. I spoke to him when we were investigating yesterday when the body was found. I have his name in my notebook. I'll find it and then we'll go check him out."

Soon afterward, Detective Jones introduced himself and his partner Detective Anders to the clerk at the Maywood Hotel. "Yesterday we spoke to a man by the name of Albert Berman, I think he was the one that wore a monocle. What can you tell us about him?"

"He's a real gentleman, retired and living on a

pension. He goes out in the morning and comes back in about four P.M. I hand him his mail and a newspaper and he reads them in the big chair by the window."

"How long has he been here and what room is he in?" asked Jones.

"His room is 712 but he's not back yet. He's been here a couple of months. Do you need me to look it up to make sure?"

"No, we'll come back when he's here. You don't need to mention we asked about him."

"Is he a suspect? You were investigating that murder here yesterday," the clerk said.

Jones said. "No, we are checking several things. I missed seeing the man with the monocle and wanted to see it for myself. Just keep our visit to yourself, please."

The detectives decided to follow Albert Berman aka. Colonel Mustard as they were calling him now, for a few days to see what he was up to with the pawn shops and jewelry stores. A team was assigned to follow him in the evenings and found out that he went out about five-thirty and walked to a restaurant for dinner. Then walked around the upscale residential areas. Saturday night they saw him enter a house. They knew the residents were gone because they saw them leave a few minutes before Albert Berman entered. They watched and waited then kept following him so the detectives could make the case when they found out about the pawn shops and jewelry stores.

Monday Jones and Anders followed him. Bank first, then lunch at the J.C. Penny's Counter and on to the 3rd Street Pawn Shop. Then he talked to the woman at Kay's Jewelers. And back to the hotel. Detective Jones said. "Those kids had his itinerary correct." They continued their surveillance until the evening officers came on duty.

Jones and Anders went back to the office and filed the papers for search warrants for the hotel and bank lock boxes.

Tuesday they went to the Maywood Hotel with the search warrants. Jones knocked on the door for room 712. Colonel Mustard answered. "Hello, how, can I help you?"

Anders said. "We have a search warrant for your room Mr. Berman."

They found nothing incriminating. Until Anders picked up the crossword puzzle book from the bedside table. He scanned the pages then, on an almost blank puzzle page an address was written. He looked closer and found similar address pages throughout the book. He showed it to his partner. Then checked the burglary addresses.

Then they went to the bank and found jewelry from several of the robberies. Mr. Albert Berman was arrested immediately and taken to the station.

Berman said, "It was self-defense, Sammy Blanky tried to kill me because I didn't get enough money for the loot from the 3rd Street Pawn Shop owner." When asked about the other pawn shops he said. "I like looking in them, I don't do any business with them."

"What about the jewelry stores?"

"I like to talk to the women there is all, they're my age. It makes the day a little better to flirt with them."

The 3rd Street Pawn Shop owner was arrested.

The Newspaper story read: "HOTEL MURDERER ARRESTED" The Colonel's photo was there. Police Detective Anders gives credit for the apprehension to a couple of young sleuths, who will remain nameless for their protection.

"Nothing about Mr. Berman looking like Colonel Mustard." Jimmy said, punching her arm playfully. "We solved our first crime, Sherlock."

"Yes, indeed, Watson." Marion said, hitting him back.

WHAT IS A MOMENT

A moment is the blink of the eye
A dot in time
A moment to remember can be
A whole scene of our life

We have good moments and bad
Joy and moments so sad
Some are fleeting moments
To be remembered forever

Moments build up to a lifetime
Maybe you are a sweet moment in someone's life
Do they bring out the memory and smile?
I hope they do and enjoy it each time

NANCY B. DAILEY

Nancy B Dailey was first published while in high school. She was always writing, but never once thought of becoming "a writer." That is, until her daughter said—many years later—"Mom, there's this lady you need to write a book about." So she did. And since she was now retired, she continued writing articles, short stories, flash fiction, and more recently, even some ghost writing. She now has two books of her own published, and is working on a third.

MY LITTLE JACK RUSSELL

111"Her name is Darlun," a deep voice said
While I lie sleeping in my bed.

Next morning dawned bright and new,
My dream returned with memories of you.

I looked on weekends at Pet Smart
For a special dog that would steal my heart.

I grew so sad for you were never there.
I wondered if I should no longer care,

And then…and then…an adopt-a-thon,..
To the local shelter I was drawn.

The room was crowded, I could not see.
A gentleman moved, and you stared at me.

A big smile spread from ear to ear,
I was so excited to find you here!

We had good times, you and I,
Throughout the years that slipped o by.

You chased the squirrels in the park.
We'd take long walks 'til it was dark.

You traveled with ne in the car
On many trips, some near, some far.

We visited friends and family,
Went geocaching in Tennessee.

You chased birds on a Florida beach,
But they always flew—just out of reach.

The memories of you bring smiles to my face,
For they are good ones that cannot be erased.

Someday we'll be together again, you'll see,
My little Jack Russell Darlun and me.

LOIS CURRAN

Lois Curran was born in Arkansas, raised in Salem, Oregon and moved to Missouri when she was 15. Writing has always been a passion, but she never made the time. However, she'd talked about it for years. Then one day her son gave her a computer, printer and some books on how to write a novel. He told her 'Mom it's time to write your book', and she did. She is now a published author and spends a lot of her time doing what she loves best – writing.

Curran is a member of Ozarks Romance Authors, American Christian Fiction Writers, and Sleuths' Ink Mystery Writers.

With years of experience as a nurse in her local health department, Curran uses real-world details to create a believable potline.

THE LAW FIRM

A lfred knew it was not going to be a good day when he saw the bloody body of J.K. Jenkins sprawled in the lobby of his law firm. He pulled shaky fingers through unruly hair, stepped back from the corpse and said through gritted teeth, "Who the hell did this?"

Three associates stepped from their offices and looked at the body.

"He wasn't there when I came in this morning," Jake the youngest member of the group said.

As if that explained anything, Alfred thought, but held his tongue as he tried to wrap his head around the sight his eyes beheld.

"Well, we're in deep trouble if we don't get him out of here." Laura, the only female attorney paced back and forth. "Everyone knows we had a nasty confrontation with this guy yesterday and Jim threatened to kill him in front of a lobby full of clients."

All four attorneys stared at J.K.'s lifeless form. An obvious puncture wound on his chest with congealed blood that covered a large portion of his shirt left little to their imaginations.

"Looks like a stab wound," Lester the quiet of the four said a little above a whisper. "But what happened to the weapon?"

"I pulled it out, cleaned off the blood, and put it back in the drawer," Jim said.

"You did what!" Laura let out a blood curdling screech. "What were you thinking? That's like an admission of guilt."

"Well, I did do it." Jim shifted his weight from one foot to the other and eyed his peers. "And you all know exactly why I had to."

"Are you on drugs? Or just plain ignorant?" Jake glared at the self-accused attorney. "You can't just fly off the handle and kill someone because they threatened to expose us."

"And what would you have done? Sit back and let him ruin our firm, our reputations, and for an extra bonus, send us to prison?"

"But murder?" Laura stood with arms akimbo. "The last I heard, killing someone could definitely land you in prison." She strode to the front door and pulled down the shade.

Alfred wished he'd never gotten out of bed this morning. In a million scenarios he could have envisioned, he never could have imagined himself in the middle of a murder cover-up. Yet he wasn't naïve, he was very aware if he refused go along with this, his law practice was doomed.

He circled the room and stood eye to eye with Jim. "Since you took it upon yourself to handle this sticky situation, do you have a plan to get this body out of our office?"

Jim shook his head. "I don't know what we're

going to do with the body. But let me assure you of one thing I do know. Our firm swindled money from J.K.s account and before we could cover it up, he figured it out. He knew we did it and there was no way we could get out of it. He was determined to ruin us."

"Oh, ya think?" Laura said. "I told you guys we couldn't get away with it. You can't steal over two million dollars and cover your tracks."

"None of that matters now." Alfred rubbed the bridge of his nose and tried to ignore a headache that threatened to settle in. "We just need to get him out of here."

"Okay," Jim said. "Let's wrap the corpse in the rug from my office and put it in my trunk. I'll figure out what to do with it later."

"Let's do it." Alfred said.

Fifteen minutes later the three guys carried the body to the rear parking lot and tucked it into the trunk of Jim's Lincoln Continental.

"That's done." Jim slammed the lid and they trekked back in the office.

"Almost got the mess cleaned up." Laura said. "I mopped with soap and water, then a bleach solution." She tossed the mop head in a trash bag. "The messy towels are all in here too. Put it in your trunk." She extended the bag to Jim and he headed out the door.

"Don't open the office until noon. I've got to figure out how to get us out of this," Alfred said and stepped inside his office, closed the door. He wondered if he'd ever feel comfortable in his establishment again. He leaned against the door and went over his options, one by one. He walked to his desk, plopped down in the chair and picked up the phone receiver.

There was only one option that made sense. Self-preservation.

He dialed a number and waited. "Police department, how could I help you?"

"I need to report a murder. And I know where they dumped the body."

SHIRLEY MCCANN

Meet Shirley McCann who is our YA author and all things spooky and mysterious. She enjoys going on ghost hunts and never fails to make the group laugh. Shirley is the author of the Amazon best-selling series, The Scarry Inn, as well as other mysteries. Her award-winning short stories have appeared in Woman's World, Alfred Hitchcock, and The Forensic Examiner, as well as numerous other publications. One was even published on a can of Coffee. Her first (but not last) romance novel, as well as her short story collections can also be found on Amazon. Shirley is a co-founder of Sleuths' Ink Mystery Writers. She also maintains memberships in The Springfield Writer's Guild and The Ozarks Romance Authors.

ANOTHER STORMY MARRIAGE

Another storm. The maple tree branch scratched across the upstairs window. Lights flickered on and off, sending a feeling of unease up Lori's spine.

What a night for David to be away. Lori hated being alone. Especially in this isolated dump David insisted they buy.

"We can flip it," he said. "That's where the money is these days. With your flair for decorating and my knowledge of construction, it's a win-win situation."

That was almost a year ago and so far David hadn't followed through on any of their renovation plans. Which is why the tree, another of David's promised projects, still scraped the house during high winds, creating that annoying, spine-tingling screech each time the wind blew. It was enough to make anyone feel on edge.

Especially when you're alone in the house.

Flip it? She'd like to flip it right into the ocean and count her losses.

Her cell phone rang, causing her to jump. "David, is that you? Are you coming home tonight?"

She bit her lip waiting for a response, but all she heard was static. That was another problem living out here. Cell service was horrible enough without the storms, but when the weather was bad, getting a signal was nearly impossible.

"David?" she screamed into the phone. "Can you hear me?"

The front door burst open slamming against a wall. Had she remembered to lock it? It didn't seal perfectly anymore unless it was locked. Another of David's unfulfilled promises.

"David?"

No answer. A gust of wind spiraled objects across the room. The lights dimmed, shrouding the room in near darkness. "Is someone there?" She aimed the phone's light toward the front door, trying to steady her racing heart as she crept closer to the sound of the banging door. From behind her a hand circled her neck and clamped across her mouth.

"Don't scream." Like she could if she wanted to. Besides, that voice sounded vaguely familiar.

"David?" It couldn't be him. David wouldn't scare her like this. She tried to remain calm, praying her husband was playing a sick joke on her.

"I'm going to remove my hand," he said. "And you're not going to scream, are you?"

She shook her head. What good would screaming do anyway? There weren't any neighbors around for miles. Another reason David insisted they buy this place. It would be their own little cozy hideaway from the rest of the world.

"Why are you doing this?" She croaked out the words, panic snaking through her body. She thought she and David were a perfect couple, but obviously she'd missed some serious problems.

"Because you were right," David whispered. His breath on her ear, usually a welcomed sensation now engulfed her in fear. "This place is a dump. And I have no clue how to fix it. I really thought I could, but it's hopeless." Lori noticed the despair in his voice. Maybe she could convince him there was still a chance, even if in her own heart she didn't believe it any more than he did.

"It's not hopeless, David. You and I? We can fix it. Just like we planned." She prayed she sounded more convincing than she really was.

"No, we can't." He spun her around so quickly, she lost her footing and fell against the fireplace. That's when she noticed the knife in his hand. "And I don't need you around to keep reminding me of what a failure I am."

"David, please." Her voice shrieked but she barely noticed it above the thunder. Flashes of angry light slashed across the room, reminding her of a horror movie. Except this was real and her husband planned to kill her.

"You're not thinking rationally," she told him. She refused to be a victim. At least not without a fight. "How will killing me get rid of the problem? The house will still be here. The problems will still be here."

He laughed, a low guttural sound that soon escalated into hysteria. "Ever heard of life insurance? I'll be able to hire someone to complete the work needed to fix this place. And then I can sell it for a nice profit."

Oh gawd! How long had he been planning this? How could she have been so blind?

She had to do something. It was useless to try and reason with a maniac with a knife.

Lori bolted for the door, her foot catching David's leg as she fled. He tripped onto the floor, but not before the knife caught Lori's right arm. A gush of blood oozed from the wound, but Lori kept running. She had no clue how she'd get away. Her car keys remained inside the house. Her only hope was to run and hide in the forest of trees that surrounded their home and hope she didn't bleed to death before she reached safety.

As if in slow motion a streak of lightning snaked across the sky and struck their house in a violent attack. Thunder roared a fierce warning. Lori stood back and watched flames of red and orange lick the house's exterior before it engulfed the entire house in blazing inferno.

Moments later sirens screamed in the distance. Medical personnel attended to Lori's wound while firefighters fought the violent flames.

"Did my husband get out?" she asked.

"I'm afraid not," the fire chief told her. "He never had a chance. It's a miracle you managed to get out when you did and with only a cut." He put his hand on her shoulder. "I'm very sorry for your loss."

No doubt the fire chief referred to the loss of her husband, but Lori's thoughts were on the house. The structure was a total loss. Now with David's life insurance, along with the homeowner's insurance, Lori could start over with a new life and a brand new home.

S. J. MAIS

Meet S. J. Mais. S. J. became interested in writing after obsessively reading romance novels once her three children were grown and there was time to spare. She started writing romance short stories and poetry and joined Ozarks Romance Authors for inspiration, camaraderie, and support. Shirlene is proud to be published in the ORA anthology. She's married to her high school sweetheart and resides in the beautiful Ozarks. Besides her writing, her five grandchildren keep her busy and she enjoys every minute of it.

THE DANCE OF ROMANCE

"There! All packed away for the summer." She smiled as she locked her classroom door and whispered, "I'm free!" No summer classes to teach or attend. Let the summer of romance begin! "Well, the summer of reading about romance anyway." Angel Ashford chuckled to herself and made her way across the street to the bookstore.

In her enthusiasm to get inside, she didn't notice the man on his way out. She glanced up just before she ran into him. She moved to her left at the same time he shifted to his right. Quickly, she stepped to the right and was all but horrified when he mirrored the movement. She took a breath and tried to make the best of the awkward moment.

"How much do I owe you for the dance lesson?" Amused green eyes peered into her hazel ones when she grinned and stepped away from him. He inclined his head and smiled, flashing twin dimples, that caused a jolt of excitement to course through her.

"It was my pleasure, no charge. Perhaps a waltz next time?" he asked over his shoulder as the door shut behind him and he walked away.

What just happened? She realized she stood there with her mouth hanging open. She snapped it shut and muttered, "Smooth, Angel, smooth. Your life is one big romantic dance with a stranger." She laughed and meandered through the store until she reached the romance section. Studying the titles, she started to pull books off the shelves.

"Did you find everything you were looking for, Angel?" Mr. Peterson said through a smile.

She let the huge pile of books drop from her arms onto the counter. "Everything except the new book by my favorite author that was supposed to available today." She really wanted that book. "It wasn't on the shelf."

"Still love a good romance I see." Mr. Peterson grinned and shook his head. "It's probably in the back waiting to be shelved. What's the title? I'll look for it." He narrowed his eyes and continued, "You know, my wife and I are retiring this summer. Our nephew is taking over the bookstore. He's tired of living in the city. Wants to settle down in a small town. To be frank, he's quite eligible. If you know what I mean." He winked and his eyes twinkled. "How about a little real-life romance? I'm sure the two of you would hit it off. I can introduce you as soon as he gets back."

She rolled her eyes at his attempt at matchmaking. He mentioned his nephew every chance he got. She grabbed her bag full of books and made a run for it before he could launch into another session of *The Bachelor*. "Thank you, Mr. Peterson, but..." She lifted the bag a little higher in the air, "I have enough romance right here in this bag to last the summer."

"I'll just have him run the book over when it's unpacked," he called out.

"That's not necessary!" She looked back and replied as she pushed through the door and ran smack into a hard chest. "Oompf" She grunted, dropped her bags and stumbled backward. Large, warm hands steadied her before she could lose her balance entirely. Unable to catch her breath when she met the green-eyed gaze of the man she'd run into earlier, she squeaked. "You!" Why did her voice sound like that?

He chuckled and before she realized what happened he'd pulled her to him. She couldn't help but smile when she found herself being waltzed about on the sidewalk. Nonetheless she was stunned speechless as he twirled her, then came to a stop. He released her and she immediately missed the warmth of his embrace. Was she crazy? All she could do was stand there while he picked up her bag and handed it to her.

"I didn't realize we would have that second dance so soon, milady. I do hope we bump into each other again. How are you at the Tango?"

He looked at her, waiting for her to say something, but all she could do was stand there, once again mouth agape. Twice she had literally run into the specimen of a man straight from the cover of a romance novel, and what did she do? Her best mute statue impersonation apparently.

"Until next time then." He winked then turned and entered the bookstore.

She made her way home smiling at the encounter she'd had with the handsome stranger. She circled through the house, dipped and swayed to the music in her head as she dusted. She imagined herself staring into his emerald-colored eyes while he dipped her low and provocatively. Then his lips met hers in a luscious ki—

The doorbell ring brought her out of her romantic fantasy and back into reality. "Who could that be?" she said to thin air. Her mind wondered back to her daydream. She couldn't believe she'd let herself go there, but the thoughts lingered as she made her way to the door.

Then she recalled Mr. Peterson said he would send his nephew over with her book this afternoon. "Great. Looks like I'm going to meet his nephew after all," she mumbled and opened the door.

Her heart jumped to her throat. "You!" She exclaimed and wondered if her fantasy still lingered and had conjured him up. She looked into his green eyes as he held the book out toward her.

"Paul Peterson, at your service, milady."

The lump in her throat went down hard when he bowed low with a flourish, then grinned at her and straightened in all his dimpled glory. Was she ever going to be able to breathe again? How could he make her feel this way?

"My uncle asked that I deliver this to you. Said you were in need of romance. I mean your romance book." His smile widened and he stepped forward. "I believe you owe me another dance."

The warmth of his closeness invaded her private space and she welcomed it. Could this be fate? She reached into the bag and pulled out the book he'd just delivered. "Funny you should mention that. Tango, wasn't it?" I showed him the book and he laughed. His dimples cut deeper into his cheeks as he read the title out loud. His voice deep and husky.

"It Takes Two to Tango."

Perhaps she wouldn't just be reading about romance this summer after all...

THE END

DRAGONS

Today's children should be taught dragons need not be feared. Dragons are totally misunderstood! I threw the rock I was clutching in my hand as far as I could and watched as it plunked into the water, ripples spreading out on the surface as it disappeared. Dragon stories have long been a favorite of mine. I've always believed dragons are real, even if I've never encountered one. Well, that I'm aware of anyways. Dragon shifters can be human after all.

"I couldn't agree more," said my date as he gathered more wood for the fire. His voice rumbled through me like thunder and I shivered.

I turned from the shore where I stood and looked over my shoulder at him. He dropped the armful of branches he had collected and started to form a teepee structure with the bigger branches around the kindling he had already prepared. Tall and lean, his muscles rippled as he effortlessly stacked branches the size of small trees. He looked up and caught me staring.

I felt the heat flare in my face, knowing it blazed as brightly as the soon to be campfire. "I didn't realize I had said that aloud," I said as I walked over to where I'd tossed my backpack and started rummaging around for some matches. "You must think me ridiculous to be talking about dragons as if they existed. Some first date, huh?" I frowned, not finding anything to light the campfire with. "Hey, I can't find any matches, did you bring any? Or are you good with rubbing two sticks together to start that fire?"

"Got it covered!" he said.

I watched as he sucked in a big breath then let loose a stream of fire that reduced the pile of wood to ashes in the blink of an eye.

He smiled, a dimple forming in his left cheek as he said, "Oops, guess I'll go gather some more wood."